Mesa Country

Jane Candia Coleman

Swallow Press/Ohio University Press
Athens

For David and Daniel
and for Glenn

99 98 97 96 95 94 93 92 91   7 6 5 4 3 2   (cloth)
99 98 97 96 95 94 93 92   7 6 5 4 3 2   (paper)

Swallow Press/Ohio University Press books are printed on acid-free paper ∞

Library of Congress Cataloging-in Publication Data

Coleman, Jane Candia
        Stories from Mesa Country / Jane Candia Coleman
        p. cm.
        ISBN 0-8040-0949-X (cloth)
        ISBN 0-8040-0957-0 (paper)
        1. Women–West (U.S.)–Fiction. 2. Western stories. I. Title.
        PS3553.047427S7   1991
        813'.54–dc20   91-4174
                                                                    CIP

Contents

Acknowledgments

This book was made possible in part by a grant from the Pennsylvania Council on the Arts.

"The Voices of Doves" is reprinted from "The Voices of Doves," fiction chapbook, winner of the Gila Review fiction award in 1986, published by Ocotillo Press, 1988, copyright, Jane Candia Coleman.

"The Paseo" appeared in *Puerto Del Sol.*

"Sunflower" appeared in *Plainswoman.* Winner of the Lois Philips Hudson Fiction Award, 1983.

"Aunt Addy and the Cattle Rustlers" appeared in *The Gila Review.*

"Acts of Mercy" appeared in *Plainswoman.*

"Mesa Country" is reprinted from "The Voices of Doves."

"Greywolf's Hoss" and "Tumbleweed" appeared in *New Frontiers, Vol. I and Vol. II,* Tor Books, 1990. (Permission to reprint granted.)

"Marvel Bird" appeared in *South Dakota Review.*

"The Ugliest Woman in the World" appeared in *Horizons West*.

"Mirage" appeared in *South Dakota Review*.

Part I. Mesa Country

Then. . .

The Voices of Doves

They are coming back from the burial ground. I can see
them walking, two abreast, along the narrow track by the
wash. Tom has his head down, his hands in the pockets of
his black suit. Beside him, Reverend Sherman is talking,
waving his arms, trying, I'd guess, to comfort. Behind them
come Enid and Faith, square shapes in best blue dresses,
and then Seth and Arch, leggy as colts, uncomfortable in
Sunday suits, in the shadow of tragedy. Now a space, long
seconds passing before I see Luisa. She is alone, walking
slowly. She is crying. I know that, even from this distance, from my bed beside the window. She wipes her eyes
on her apron. Her shoulders heave. She has been crying
for three days.

I wish I could shout so they could hear me. I wish the
Reverend would go to her, assure her of her place in heaven
and in our house. I wish one of them, Tom or the children,
would take her by the arm, lead her home. Instead they act
as if she is not there at all, perhaps thinking that if they ignore her she will vanish and with her this hour, these three
days, the newly turned earth in the far field.

Well, they are wrong. None of it will disappear. We'll live with it, tiptoe around it, make excuses and blame each other. And who is to blame? Tom, for coming here to homestead at the foot of the red rock mountains? For begetting children upon my body? Sons to inherit, daughters to marry? Or I, in my—not innocence, that's not the word I want—my cocoon, my shroud of womanhood that brought me here, a continent away from home to wifehood, motherhood, acceptance of death as part of life? Birth and death are what I see and take for granted. Life comes and goes with the seasons, with the years. There is a violence in this soil, in the people who labor on it. Perhaps it is only the truth of earth, and one accepts it or goes down in defeat.

Of course we will all blame Luisa. She is Mexican, a servant. She cannot read, neither her language nor ours, and those few words of English that she speaks are self-effacing. Yet she has held my life and my children's in her hands, and they are good hands, filled with compassion. Seven times now she has helped me give birth; four living children, two born dead, and this last, this last. Ah, but how could she have known? How, in her ignorance, could she have known?

I can hear them now, muffled voices, booted footsteps on the porch. Reverend Sherman says he will come in to me, the mother, the bereaved. But I will pretend to be asleep, realizing this moment, clear and quick like sun after a rain cloud, that I do not like this man, this preacher of God's word. He has talked sin and damnation so long he's forgotten the rest: the soul's need for warmth, the body's for expression, the hunger of all of us for forgiveness. He should learn compassion from Luisa, but to him, in his narrowness, she does not exist.

She is in the kitchen now, crying out, "Ay! Ay!" And the cook, the woodcutter's wives who have come to help prepare the food, surround her with their soft language, with quick flutterings of hands. "Shhh. Shhh." I hear them, the voices of doves.

Tom taps at the door. I close my eyes. Right now I do not love him, either. There have been too many children, too many dead. I do not want to see his hands, fists in his pockets, or his eyes, bewildered, blaming, asking whose mistake it was. Right now I want to be left alone, to gather myself. Out here a woman cannot succumb to weakness, cannot weep where she can be seen. Too many lives are dependent on us, though they do not know it, these men, these ranchers and woodcutters, trappers and prayer-makers. These prospectors and bounty hunters who storm the brothels, take the Indian girls in the fields, quickly and in silence.

Well, it is the way of life. They come to us for comfort and survival and for sons. And now there is one son who will never be.

There is no comfort in me in this moment. I am cold and dry, a husk thrown to the animals, feeling nothing. I am tired of all of them, their hungers and demands. I *will* sleep, letting myself go into nothing while they eat the food and say words that do no good at all. . .

It's morning. I can tell because the shadows still lie in the folds of the mountains, and there is a stirring in the kitchen and smoke rising from the woodcutter's tents. And there is Enid running across the fallow field, sturdy as a small tree. I should do something to curb her wanderings I know, but she is a determined child. And she loves this place in a way I cannot. Already, at twelve, she knows every flower, every trail. The Mexicans spoil her, give her gifts, invite her to share their suppers. The Indians speak to her though they ignore everyone else. And, I admit, if I have a favorite child it is this one, stubborn, blue-eyed. This land is in her bones. She loves it despite its hardness, its cruelty. She and Arch are alike this way. I think they would kill for this place, and kill again. They fight each other constantly, quick flashes of temper, of passion, eyes crackling like thunderstorms.

"Enid!" Arch said last week. Was it only last week? It

seems a year. "Enid! She's so ornery she ought to be put out of her misery."

And we all laughed and then comforted Enid who was stamping her foot and holding back tears. She was *not* ornery, she said. She had only tried to ride Arch's new spotted gelding and had been bucked off three times before she'd been caught at it. "I want my own horse," she cried. "One of my own."

And Arch had said, "Fool girl. Just don't spook mine again."

There's too much love in her. Given a horse of her own she'll cherish it and forget everything else. "You'll never get a lick of work out of her," Tom says. "Give her a horse and she'll be off in those mountains after the Indians day and night."

It's true, I know. But I'd give her one if I could. I'd let her have a tame creature to pet instead of the half-dead beasts of the fields that she brings home to nurse.

"Mama!" She peers around the door. Her eyes are round and so bright they startle. She brings life into this room that has known, so recently, suffering and death. Her body pulses with it, and her hands, filled with flowers.

"Look what I brought," she says. She sits on the foot of the bed with a small thump. I have never been able to teach her to move gracefully. Perhaps out here it is unnecessary. Out here strength is the greatest aid to a woman. Men don't look for tender blossoms. They seek out endurance.

"It's butterfly weed," she says. "There's a whole field of it. I saw it yesterday at the funeral." She looks at me, wondering if she should have spoken of it.

"It's all right," I tell her. "It's over now. Done."

"It isn't." She squirms, draws her legs up under her. "It's not over. Luisa won't get out of bed. She says she's waiting to die because of what she did. She says she's got too old to birth babies, and that it was a sign. She's not even crying, Mama. She's just lying there."

This last child came hard. Hard and for nothing. It took two days before I saw him, round, perfect, bawling like a calf before Luisa began to wash him and made her mistake. Such a small error to be so final. Tom had all the medicine bottles lined up in order for her, he thought. Luisa can't read, but she knows the order of those bottles. Hands flying, she can make a mother comfortable in moments, gather up a child and show it tenderness, clean it, wrap it tight.

I test my own strength, tighten the slack muscles of legs and thighs. I am bleeding as if my heart is broken and pours out. My breasts ache with unused milk. I'll have to do something about that soon, but I must try to get up, to go to Luisa. She must not be allowed this weakness, this wish for death.

"Help me," I say to Enid. "Hand me my robe."

She puts down her flowers with care. Her fingers linger on the lace of the robe. It is the last piece of finery I have, brought from St. Louis, God, so long ago. This and my own mama's pearls, wrapped in a scarf in my drawer. Enid loves them. Begs to see them, looks at them as if they are a mirror or a glimpse of something else, something beautiful and sweet, untainted by this reality.

"Where're your dad and the boys?"

"Gone out. Running Wolf came in at first light and said a fence was down and the cattle were all over the mountain."

They'll be gone a long time. A cow and a calf can disappear in a minute. There are a thousand ravines, blind canyons, trails that vanish into the wilderness. Rounding them up can take days.

I slide from the bed, feel the gushing of blood. Enid slips her arm around me, braces for my weight. She is solid and warm, a rock in the sun. Here is one who will survive. Who will take the joys and the sorrows and thrive like a weed, a thorny cactus filled with sweet water.

"Come on, Mama," she says. "Lean harder."

I will. She can take it, this little one who talks to plants, who has learned the languages of Indians and Mexicans without realizing there are any differences. Her shoulders are wide, her arms always open. Where will it take her, all this knowledge, this feeling for others?

The tiles are cool on my feet. Thank God for them, for a real floor after the packed earth I swept and wrestled with in my first years: dust, insects, stinging scorpions that still live in the walls so we must watch always, shake out blankets and shoes and pieces of clothing, and have the women to patch the adobe every year. They come with their buckets of clay and their trowels and scaffolding and fill the cracks and smooth the mud with sure strokes. Sometimes they sing and I listen, and sometimes dance to their rhythms, alone, unwatched, my body speaking for me.

What would the Reverend Sherman think, or Tom, if they could see me dancing, stretching my arms to shadows? Well, they have never seen me, never will. I have my world, my dreams. They help. A little. Out here, one uses any weapon to fight the loneliness. Even a solitary dance with a broomstick, the sound of a voice singing.

Maria the cook rushes at me scolding. I am out of bed too soon, she says. She runs for a chair, a towel to fold as a cushion. And now I am here, I should eat. An egg, fresh bread, coffee with sugar and milk. Her hands fly like her tongue. I have upset her, appearing like a pale ghost of myself in her doorway. The food tempts me. I cannot remember having eaten at all these last days, but I must have. Or have I only slept?

"Yes," I say to her round face. "Yes. I'll eat. But first I want to see Luisa."

"Luisa. Ay!" She wails at me. Luisa is lying with her face to the wall on a cot behind the stove. She is waiting to die.

I shuffle across the room, find her shriveling before my eyes, wrinkled and parched like the skin of a toad.

I stand here. I don't know what to say. We share the same burden, the same grief. We have labored together,

she and I, over a child, and whose body is now the more
ripped by pain, mine or hers? She who oiled the skin of the
newborn with carbolic acid, and with me watched helpless
as he burned to death.

Is one pain different from another? I don't know. I only
know that it comes and we bear it, in silence digging our
nails into our flesh, or crying out as these women do. But
they do not all grieve openly. I have looked in their faces
and seen quiet anguish there. I have seen them in the
town, in the church, praying and lighting candles and walking slowly, holding in some nameless suffering as Luisa
does now, hugging herself with arms that have been strong
when I was weak.

She looks at me. Her mouth opens, but no sound comes.
She has few teeth left, so I look into darkness. They age
early, these women. I think she is not much older than I,
but worn by wind and sun and clutching at life. Even my
own teeth are going. "For every child a tooth," they say.
Well, it comes on us. We cannot stop it, but we need not
seek it out, either.

I don't know how to say this to her. The guilt is, after all,
hers. My head is swimming. I kneel by the small bed.
"Luisa," I say, "you mustn't do this. You must get up. Eat.
Live. We need you. I need you. There is so much milk. So
much blood. I don't know what to do. And there will be
more babies, and me here alone."

Yes, more babies. Time in a month or so to begin another; to submit. That's what it is now. Submission. Filling up
like a clay jar. What I need is wisdom. Someone to share
the burden. Someone whose memory is long, who can
show me the way.

I put my hands on her shoulders, feel her bones like the
broken wings of Enid's dove in its woven cage on the porch.
"Listen," I say to her, angry now, impatient with her lack of
response. "Listen. It's your people who built this place, this
house. Who have lived on this land forever. It's your women

who made the houses and the missions, who know how to survive no matter what. Are you going to disgrace them? Your people?"

Something moves in her eyes—a memory, a triumph. I shake her. She rattles like a gourd.

"I need you to show me. Do you understand? I need someone to help. To show me, too."

Enid leans over, speaks in Spanish, her voice rising and falling like music, like water rushing in the wash. She begins to cry, her tears spattering across the old woman's face. She stamps her foot, and now her words crack like a whip, lethal, angry.

Luisa sighs. There is relief in the sound, and defeat. She pulls up the wasted corners of her mouth.

"Get up!" Enid shouts, blue eyes blazing like wildfire. "Now! Silly old woman. My mother needs you. I need you."

Luisa mumbles, crosses herself. She moves as slowly as I have moved, feeling her way back into sunlight. We look at each other across a culture, across a grave. Neither, I see, makes a difference. It is survival that is important. And dignity. And caring for one another in a wilderness. Enid knows. Far better than I, she knows.

"What did you say to her?" I ask.

And she says, simply, "Everything."

"Bruja," Luisa says. "Witch." She puts her arms around us both at once, and we stand linked, filled with hunger for something we cannot name, known only in our memories, in our blood, in our hands that build and gather, in our bodies that insure continuity, in our hearts that understand the sudden calling of the dove.

Tumbleweed

Pinal, Arizona 1888. . .

The sun beat down upon the tin roof of the shack, heedless of its inhabitants. There were only two: a woman who lay as if drugged on the bed, and a man who stood buttoning his trousers.

"Bring me some whiskey, will you?" she said, her voice thick. "The money's on the shelf."

He reached over her head and counted the coins, and she opened her eyes and watched him. They were flat eyes, the color of the silver. "Don't take more'n you need," she said. "The last son of a bitch stole my bracelet."

"Who was it?" He counted a few coins into his callused palm. "You want me to find him?"

She shook her head, rolling it slowly back and forth as if it hurt her to move. "Who knows?" she said. "It was dark anyhow."

The heat rolled over him, and the stench. He was not fastidious, miners couldn't be, but the airlessness, the stink of bodies caught him suddenly, and the sight of the limp figure below him. "Get up," he said. "Come on out, Mattie. I'll buy you a drink. No sense layin' here."

She moved her head again, the faded curls made dark by sweat. "Just get the whiskey. I'm not going any place except to heaven. This here's hell, you know." She laughed, short and sharp like a fox.

He clamped his hat to his head and opened the door, letting in the wind, the dust, a glimpse of sky, hard blue enamel and cloudless. "Be right back," he said.

"That's what they all say." She closed her eyes again and lay still.

And wasn't it true? Hadn't they all promised, and hadn't she always been left? She, Mattie, excited, eager, and then finally without eagerness at all except the wish to stop waiting. Because whatever they said was a lie. Whatever they told you—the boys, the mothers, the madams, the men—it was a lie.

Hadn't he said it, too, at the train from Tombstone on that last, dreadful morning—Wyatt with his panther-colored hair and his eyes the steady blue of a hunting cat's?

"Please hurry," she'd said in answer. "Please hurry home." And she'd slipped her arms around his lean waist, felt him stepping back, away from her fear, her needs.

They'd been a mismatch from the start. She knew that now, but the fact didn't keep her from wanting him. Or from hating him, either. And she didn't know which was worse.

In the darkness behind her lids he danced, out of reach, unknowable, elusive as always, and she with her hunger like a cancer, growing bigger and bigger, blotting out thought. . .

Tombstone, Arizona October, 1881. . .

She lay in bed in the house on Fremont Street listening to the wind and the howling of coyotes. She wished she could howl like that—like the devil himself—shrill, high, piercing. She wished she could run, a grey shadow, to the house where they lay together, the city whore with her long hair, and Wyatt, his cool blue eyes warming at the sight of white flesh.

Mattie curled her hands into fists. There was no way she could sleep with the coyotes, the music and shouting from the streets, the saloons and dance halls, her own thoughts rising faster than she could sort them. She got up, shook out her skirts, opened the door and went out and down the porch to Allie's, remembering as she went all the nights that she and Allie had spent together, many of them filled with laughter, for Allie was quick-witted, quicker tongued.

"Let me in!" she shouted, pounding on the rough boards. "Let me in, Allie!"

Allie looked no bigger than a mesquite twig in her night-gown. Her eyes shone in the shadows, dark, worried. "He not back yet?" She stepped aside to let Mattie enter, then barred the door.

"No he's with her. That damned whore."

"Pot calling the kettle black," Allie said, then relented at the look on Mattie's face. "You want a drink?"

Mattie shook her head, stared at her hands balled into fists. They were big hands, fit for a farmer, suntanned and cracked. Once they'd known how to please him. She knew they had. Or had he only wanted to lose himself awhile, forgetting the first wife buried under the long grass of the Missouri prairie? Had he only lunged, headstrong bull, into the first woman he saw, sweeping her along in a desperate rush, and her captivated by his yellow hair, his cool eyes that rarely smiled, the wordlessness in the heat of their joining?

"He hasn't come home for ten days," she said.

Allie sat down at the table opposite her, the lamp between them casting a blue light. "He'll come back. She's just a play thing's all. They've never seen one like her so they got to go sniff like a pack of hounds."

"And her in season." Mattie slammed the table. "I thought we'd get here and it'd be different. A town and us both in it, not me left out on the farm on that damned prairie wondering."

"He's got work to do," Allie said. "You can't expect him around all the time."

"Once in awhile I can. Just so's I can hold my head up when I go out. Just so's they won't gossip. 'There goes poor Mattie Earp,' they say. I can feel it." Her voice rose, her red hair gathered sparks from the lamp and shone. "You know it's true, Allie! Damn it! You know."

Allie poured whiskey into a glass and pushed it across the table. "Hush up," she said, "or the whole town'll know for sure." Then she softened as she always did at the sight of Mattie helpless, on the verge of tears and temper. "God knows I'm glad he ain't mine," she said. "Your trouble is, all you do is yell and him quiet as those hills out there. It'd do you both good could you just talk once in awhile."

"Virge and Morg got all the talk in the Earp family," Mattie said. "Him—well, you just said it. He thinks. I can't stand a thinkin' man!" She was shouting again.

"Better'n a dead one."

"Is it?" Mattie lifted the glass and tossed off the contents. "All I see of him, he might as well be dead, and me with him."

"It is. Now, you bed down with me tonight. Things'll look better come morning. They always do."

The whiskey warmed her. It was a cold night, and the wind whirled at the door, the windows, the cracks in the walls. It sounded like the coyotes, like the words inside that she couldn't get at, get out; shapeless things that rose and beat at her throat where they stopped and only anger came.

Did the city whore have words? she wondered. And laughter? Was she even now lying there spent and soft, words spilling out like perfume?

She lay on the bed beside Allie's small body and stared into the dark until the darkness inside her melted into it, and she slept.

The morning was cold, the air filled with the scent of mesquite fires, a touch of frost from the Dragoon Mountains that lifted pink shoulders against the East. Clouds cut the brilliance of sky, making blue shadows.

She stood a moment on the porch watching, waiting for something to happen, something that came to her like a breath on the wind. She'd always had an instinct, feelings that formed elusive as dust devils dancing, but always, after them, came change. Time and again she'd felt this stirring and waited, wordless, for the sky to open, for life to double back on itself leaving her helpless. She tasted the air, but it told her nothing. Then she went home, poked up the fire, and put on the coffee pot.

She no longer bothered to wash or fuss with her dress, her hair. What use? No one ever looked. Wyatt came and went freely, bound on his man's errands, and she no more to him than a chair, a table, a pair of hands.

Outside the town scurried, rushed, clopped. It was never still, even at night. The mines were always open, shifts going on and off, the saloons and dance halls keeping pace. A freight wagon passed, and two burros loaded with wood. Everything passed this house near the edge of town. Everyone passed, but no one stopped. Only the light-footed Allie and Morg's wife Lou, as golden, as beautiful as a honey pot. After ten years in the family she still felt the outsider, neither beautiful nor clever, and often angry, smothering the coals of it lest it flare and destroy her.

She drank her coffee and sat staring at the floor boards. They were gritty with the sand that blew off the high desert, off the streets with their never-ending traffic.

Be damned to this place! she thought. There was a wickedness in it that came out of the ground with the silver. A pity they'd ever dug the first mine, that the place hadn't been left to the cactus, the coyotes, the Apaches.

For years she'd been following along, working the farm, helping out while Wyatt tended to his businesses—gambling with Jim, real estate, mining, timber, and finally, the law. She'd shrugged when he won and when he lost, moved on with him and the family when they succumbed to their itchy feet, because what else was there for her to do, where was there to go except with him, with them? But now when she looked at him she saw a man gone beyond her reach, a stranger whose desires were not hers. He had the distances in him, and dreams, like a young man. And she? What she dreamed of now was a house with doors, windows, a good stove and her man beside it.

She'd tried, God knew. In all the ways that had worked before, she'd tried. Except she'd never been pretty, and she'd coarsened now, stood square-shouldered and heavy-hipped, a horse that had been hitched to the plow for years, eyes fastened on the row ahead, unable to follow anything else.

"Leave off, Matt," he'd say, backing away from her arms. And more than once of late, "Best spend the night with Allie. I'll be gone awhile, and the town's not safe."

The last time she'd searched his face for a sign that he cared. What she saw was that he was already gone from her, tracking the rustlers who'd held up the stage; that he had *her* on his mind—the girl from San Francisco, her lushness barely covered by her gowns, her hunger covered by nothing at all.

"Be careful," she said, frightened by the thought of losing him, of being left. She reached out, wanting his strength.

He hugged her then, quickly, as if she stood in his way. "Bar the door," he said and went through it, a lean shadow, boot heels clicking on the porch and then, dully, in the dust of the street.

Bar the door be damned! she thought. She wished she had a man, any man to take away the emptiness, to bring back her youth and the feeling that something wonderful was about to happen, that life was out there at the edge of the prairie, and she'd find it if only she moved fast enough, loved hard enough, her red hair springing from her head with a fire of its own.

She got up and went out into the yard, her eyes on the street. When the man came past she smoothed her hair, picked up a bucket and filled it from the pump. Then she staggered under its weight.

"Please," she called to him. "Can you help me get this in the house?"

He took off his cap and looked at her while she prayed for anonymity. It would be so much easier that way.

"Eh?" he said. Then he spoke, a stream of words she couldn't grasp except that they reminded her of her youth, of a boy whose voice had been golden with promise that turned out to be lies.

Better this way. A foreigner who couldn't tell. She gestured at the bucket, at the house, and smiled, showing her teeth.

He smiled back, bowed once, and came through the gate, hand extended. He had black hair, she saw, but he wasn't young. No boy but a man come to wrest his fortune from the dark holes in the earth.

She led the way, swaying her heavy hips, looking over her shoulder to be sure he saw and followed. The rest was easy. She'd learned the tricks long ago, and out here it didn't matter that you had aged early, that you hadn't bothered to bathe. Man's world it was, but a woman's, too. Once in awhile. For a little time. She held him in her and laughed.

The shooting began, intensified, then stopped, leaving a silence made deeper by echoes that came back from mud walls, from the valley and the rock-faced mountains. A few seconds later it began again, this time deliberate, spaced, as if each shot were aimed.

She sat up, her heart beating in her ears. She rolled the man away from her and stood, tugging at her skirt.

"Who? Who?" he said, dazed by her quickness.

"You sound like a damned hoot owl," she said. "Git now! Hurry up!" She hauled at him, pushing, prodding. "Damn fool," she said. "Move!"

He stumbled out the back, and she headed for the street, forgetting her shawl, her bonnet, her shame.

"What happened?" she asked.

A man shook his head. "Dunno, lady."

"Street fight," said another. "Clantons, McLaurys, the Earps and the Holliday feller."

She stopped. "Killed?"

"Dunno."

What if Wyatt lay dying? What had she done? She stood, afraid to move. Ahead of her she saw Allie swept like a butterfly, her blue skirt ballooning in the wind, and Lou, slower, yellow hair slipping from its bun as she elbowed her way through the crowd.

She saw Doc a little way off, and then she saw the bodies. She couldn't count them, couldn't focus. She saw Allie kneel, and then Lou, and a scream froze in her throat. Not here, she thought. Not here in this godawful place. Not yet. I'm not ready yet. And she didn't know what she meant or that she thought at all.

A cart with bodies in it came toward her. It was pulled by men, not horses, and Allie ran alongside, her small face set, her arm around Lou.

Mattie moved. "What?" she said. "In God's name, what?"

"See for yourself!" Allie snapped first, out of habit. "Wyatt's alright. Virge got it in the leg, but Morg's bad. Come on. He'll need the three of us." She grabbed Mattie's arm with her free hand and moved her from her trance, but not before Mattie saw the hatless girl running blindly across the street and up to the tall figure walking there. Not before she saw how the girl stood, body arched as if she offered it, on the street, the blood and dust behind her.

In the weeks that followed she often caught herself wishing Wyatt had been shot, that it was he lying in the bed quiet under her hands like Morg or cussing a blue streak like Virge. She'd have him then—his person, his gratitude, the door closed on the bitch who could howl in the street but never come in because she, Mattie, had him, owned him, loved and hated him.

She wished it when Wyatt moved all of them to the hotel for safety, and again six months later when they stepped on the train bound for Tucson and California, with Morg cold in his box in the baggage car and Virge, holding his useless arm close to his body. Wyatt, his eyes turned to ice, saw them off. She wished he were dead because dead he'd be hers, no one else's. Dead, she could grieve for herself.

"I'll come when I'm finished here," Wyatt said.

She held to him, regardless of his impatience, of the cold wind that tugged at her skirt, her bonnet, her heart.

His words had been, of course, a lie. You were born empty and you stayed that way, and the men who came couldn't fill the space. There was too much of it, like the prairie. It was in you, around you, a darkness you carried and tried to ignore, but in the end it swallowed you like a grave.

She wished Allie were here now with her quick feet, her laughter. Odd how she missed Allie more than the rest. At times it seemed as if Allie were the part of herself that was missing, that she'd been born without, like an empty bowl, a buffalo wallow, a dip in the prairie. Once Allie had said that she wanted roses on her grave, even if she died in the middle of Kansas. Well, maybe she'd get them. As for herself, she'd have cactus, tumbleweed. She was like them, those dry and fragile things that blew outside the door.

God, she was dry! Where was he with that whiskey?

Where were they all? They'd eluded her, left her thorny with wanting. And what had it been that she wanted so much, that had danced always just on the edge of her vision like a marsh light, that had lured her on, kept her going?

There was dust in her throat. She snarled, fighting for breath. She lifted her hands, stopped, touched her breasts, one and then the other, astonished at their smallness, like gourds dried in the sun.

When the man pushed open the door and came to stand beside her, she lifted her head and stretched out her arms. "Give me," she said. "Give me. Quick."

*   *   *   *   *

Pinal, Arizona, July 7, 1888. . . "Mattie Earp, a frail deni-zen of Pinal, culminated a big spree by taking a dose of laudanum, on Tuesday, and died from its effects. She was buried on the 4th." From the *Arizona Enterprise*.

The Paseo

They still play in the plaza, those little girls in their brilliant dresses. The wind from the mountains scoops their skirts, and they laugh, twirl in it, hold down the billows mockingly as if they have something beneath that must not be exposed.

But one of them knows that soon she will have something to protect. She knows they will all grow tall and deep and holy, their bodies more precious than life. They will parade this plaza slowly, erect under the eyes of men, conscious of the pearls they bear in their darkness, conscious of sin, desirous of its consequences.

It is serious business, the paseo. In its prescribed motion the courses of lives are altered. It is a giant marketplace offering not the chilies, blankets, jars, moccasins, jewelry of the weekday trade, but the bodies, the souls of women which have no price but which are, nonetheless, bartered over, traded, moved from one owner to the other. And the women go eagerly or not so eagerly, wrapped around their pearls like oysters secreting splendor. They go, they grow old, they die, and their daughters practice the promenade, shriek in the wind, hold down dresses that wish to be wings.

The world runs on paradox. We wall up beauty behind adobe, then snarl and howl in the wilderness outside. We make animals of the least of us by telling him he is man, turn little girls into spiritual vessels at a time when honest laughter is precious, the light in their eyes beyond price.

I know. I am as guilty as any, though once I was only observer, recorder of lives and scenes. I have been in this mud city for years painting pictures, watching, listening, taking no part in the pageant, though I had my chances. Not long ago I was yellow-haired, considered handsome.

But to be bound up in that ritual would have been to lose some vitality I needed in my fingers, my heart. I chose, instead, to be father of mountains, of distances, of colors changing on the space of the desert. I was not free, but neither was I bound by voices, bodies, demands, only by my own urgings, my own needs. Another paradox, it seems. We suckle freedom in our mother's milk, yet when we escape from her we are bound to another.

These are things I think about in the night when I cannot see to paint, or when, as now, I think of the children, the little girls from the convent who walk and dream in the dust of the plaza. Once I walked among them. Now I, too, am walled behind adobe, cast out into the desert.

One child in particular attracted me. There was an aura of the unbreakable about her. I thought that the nuns would have a hard time convincing her of her guilt for original sin, that her mother, the widow who takes in boarders and who looks at me now with suspicion and disgust, would find it difficult to give her in marriage. The child, Dolores, would not be given. She would, instead, bestow herself like a queen as she bestowed on me her smiles. On me, El Chamiso. That is what she called me—after the yellow weed whose flowers hang, grey and drying on their stems all winter.

In the days before my fall, I talked to her often. I would go out and sit in the plaza on afternoons when I grew tired of my own company, of the voices of solitude. I would sit and let the giggles and gossip of little girls fly over me, would let her approach, dark eyes dancing in pointed face, aware of her daring, filled with mischief, yet already powerful, already the Queen followed by her handmaidens, giving audience to one man whose hair hung on his head like a winter weed, who revived in the presence of young laughter, who straightened to receive the honor of her attention.

Why was I not painting? she wanted to know the first time. Why was I there (jester in her court) when the snow had melted in the hills, the mountains stood up clear against the sky? The town, it seemed, marked its calendar by my comings and goings.

I told her I was growing too old to brave the winds of March. That I would wait for May, for the apples' time of blooming, and then I would pack my burro with brushes and paint and be off into the high country.

She came closer then, put one hand on my knee in a gesture so childish yet so womanly I felt my heart leap in my chest, and even, God help me, a stirring in my loins.

What was it like, that high country? she asked. And why could I not paint it from the images stored behind my eyes?

Her innocence could not recognize her words as a giving. When I began to tell her that the edges of memory are blurred, that what we recall is never what was there but only what we wish, she drew away, scornful that her gift had gone unnoticed. She ran, handmaidens behind her, small feet flashing under her striped skirt.

"El Chamiso!" she shouted from the far corner of the plaza where swirls of dust obscured her, made her brave. And they laughed, all of them, twittering like the sparrows that hide in the walls from the wind. But I did not mind. I am not bothered by names. One is as good as nother, and besides, was it not a title bestowed by a Queen?

Soon, though, I discovered her curiosity. She had never, in twelve years, been beyond the limits of the city, and she wanted to know about the world she had imagined. So I told her stories of the Indians in their pueblos, about how the desert looks in bloom. I told her of the beauty of loneliness with only the mesas for company, of the madness that came upon me when I tried to capture them on canvas. I talked to her as a man rarely talks to a woman, and she drank my words.

I waited in the plaza for them to come in a gaggle from school, moving clockwise as if in practice, though their steps were neither slow nor decorous and their voices high-pitched, carrying. Some days I brought candy–peppermint, licorice, rock crystals, or those fiery little red drops that scorch the throat, the tongue as surely as chiles. How she sucked the air after one of those! How I watched her, absorbing her pain! I wished to take her in my arms, little queen that she was, to apologize, to learn her quiverings, her stillness.

Regardless of what they say about me now, I wanted only to hold childhood in my hands, to capture her in those moments before she turned woman, aware of self, body, games of pride. I wanted the pure vitality of that female animal to enter me, to come to me so that I could know it with these hands that have failed to capture what my eyes so clearly see.

Who has ever painted time? Arrested it? No one of whom I know, though many have tried. Day after day I have gone into the desert, have seen it, luminous and living before me, have mixed my colors and begun, only to find it changed and changing again. To paint them is to indulge in mimicry, a hopeless attempt to possess what cannot be owned. It is enough to drive one mad.

And so I sat, longing for the reality of that thin body between my hands, wanting the scent of hot young breath upon my face, the dazzle of tears. Wanting anything from her that spoke of living, that was unchanged for a day, an hour, a moment.

"You're wicked," she said, looking up at me in anger. Her lip trembled as she spoke, and I lost myself in its smoothness, in the perfection of color, pale rose like a petal. I saw it in a year, grown seductive; in twenty, cracked

and dried from the sun; in forty, slack with dying. Inside
myself I wept.

"Wicked," she repeated. I had tempted her like the ser-
pent. I had burned her mouth and must do penance, make
reparation.

"What?" I asked her. "What must I do?"

She thought awhile, still and perfect between my knees,
and then her mouth curved, her eyes danced. Every day
for a week, she said, I must bring candy. Sweet candy of
wonderful colors. And for her alone. Was that not a good
penance?

I pretended to consider, nodding, weighing the thought
like a fool, and all the time watching her delight. I noticed
that her hair, which I had thought black, had fire in it, was
overlaid by a sheen of gold. Beneath its tendrils her face
shone as if under a halo.

It was then that the idea came to me. It was an honest
one and innocent. Truly. I wanted to capture that face on
canvas. I wanted to paint that child on the brink of womanhood, the lily opening, hesitant, doomed, impelled by the
fact that it lives. I wanted to paint that moment of trust
when we believe that because we are, life will not fail us. I
wanted back my own moments of certainty.

I nodded at her. "Yes," I said. "It's a good penance. I'll
do it. But you must do something for me."

She was smiling, victorious. "What?" she asked. "What,
viejo?"

Old one. To her I was the old one, not the youth she
would someday meet, watch under lowered lids in the cir-
cle of the paseo, lure to her side like a dark moth.

"You must ask your mama if I may paint you. Your por-
trait. Just as you are now."

I watched the idea grow in her, her enormous, slanted
eyes catching fire like valleys in the dawn. I watched dis-
mayed, as the first glimmer of self-consciousness touched
her and she began to view herself as an object of desire.

I cursed myself for my foolishness. No matter that in a

year or two it would have come on its own. Like the ser-
pent, I had placed knowledge squarely before her who believed in paradise.

When she spoke, her voice was still the clear treble of a
young bird, but I was not fooled. The body speaks its own
language, and hers had drawn inward, defensive, aware.

"Paint me?" she asked. "Why me?"

Why, indeed? "Never mind," I said. "It was a foolish notion. Go and play, and I'll bring you candy tomorrow."

But she was not now to be put off by promises of treats;
perhaps never again. "But I would like it," she said. "You'd
make me beautiful, and everyone would see and talk about
me."

Dreams galloped in her. I could feel them. Her hand was
on my knee, insistent. "I'll hang on the wall like a great
lady," she said, moving closer. "Please. I would like it. I will
sit still for hours and hours, and not ask for candy. I will ask
my mother tonight. I will tell her it is an honor." Her fingers
tightened. "Please."

I thought that, after all, I was not an old man. Only ma-
ture. Only tired of wrestling abstractions from the unyield-
ing body of earth. Perhaps it was time to come to terms
with the beast within; to forget lines, shapes, colors, and
learn the reality of the flesh.

I had already done the damage. I would paint her. I
would make her beautiful as, indeed, she was, and I would
make her conscious of me. Then, perhaps in a year, I
would join the others, circling her, as much a dog as they.

So dreams galloped also through me. So I, too, lost my
innocence that clear day with the glitter of March around
us and the wind from the mountains tasting of snow.

But in this town nothing is secret. Gossip leaches from
the walls. News is flashed by smiles, gestures, chance words,
as if, beneath the surface, all are fastened together, a huge
root with a thousand branches.

By the next morning, Luz, the silent woman who cooks
for me, keeps my clothes in order, comes silently to my
bed on those nights when the mountains bear down too

heavily to sleep alone, by morning Luz had heard of my simple request. Her disapproval squared the shape of her body beneath her shawl and skirt.

Her wordlessness makes her valuable as a servant, as a vessel in my bed, yet there have been times, and this was one, when her unvoiced emotions erect a wall of guilt so thick I cower before it. I could not think what I had done to earn her disapproval. I thought I would never understand women though I lived another fifty years.

They are the implacable arbiters of our behavior, demanding obedience to rules never spoken, never thought of until, in the breaking of them, we are brought up short against the impenetrable barrier of female wrath.

I pushed my dish away. "Out with it," I said harshly, seeking dominance through bluster. "What've I done?"

She folded her arms across the boulders of her breasts, the proclaimer of destiny. Under their lids, her eyes were the edges of knives. "Not what you have done," she corrected. "What you intend."

"What?"

"You would disgrace that child," she said. "You would paint her. Dishonor her. Who would have her then? How could you think such a thing could be done?"

"Disgrace?" I said. "There's no disgrace. I wish to paint her. Do I disgrace the desert by painting it? Or the houses of the city? Where's the disgrace in that, eh?"

"Who will have her," she repeated. "After she has been here in your house? After you have taken her body and put it on your canvas for everyone to see? About you and me they say nothing. About you and this child, they say, HOW COULD YOU DARE!"

I slammed my fist on the table. The dishes jumped. The milk in the jug spilled over. I roared at her, taking refuge in the falseness of the accusation. "Her face! I wanted to paint her face, you fools!"

"So you say." She was quite calm. Male rage was as nothing to her. "But the face would not be enough, eh? The face is only a door to be opened."

"You're crazy. All of you." Pain struck me at the thought of what I had loosed. I stood up. She looked at me untouched by my emotions. "You didn't say that to her? You didn't tell that child I would paint her naked?"

The look in her eyes told me I was doomed. "Yes we told her. She is almost a woman. She had to know."

I wanted to put my hands around the square golden column of her throat. I wanted her to pay—for my sin, for hers, for the deadly flower that is the world. I imagined it; the cutting edges of her eyes gone dull; her breasts running lifeless down her belly. I imagined for one moment only that I could obliterate the twining evils of religion, superstition, culture with a motion of my hands.

As if outside myself, I saw the symbolism of the act, the ritual struggle. I saw the paseo, the game of widening circles played out in this valley, in a million valleys. I saw the children of the world doomed to capitulate to the cycle. I saw men like myself who believed they were free.

"Bitches," I cried. "All of you! Evil, wicked bitches!" I let her go with such force that she fell against the table, hissing at me like a mountain cat.

I turned from her and ran, cutting across the plaza, scattering the little girls, the gentle sparrows. She was there, her eyes wide, her hands crossed over her breast like a shield.

I saw her but did not stop. Like the animal I am, I went to earth, back to the succor of the desert, where life exists in beauty and in barrenness, lays the bones of *penitentes* bare.

Aunt Addy and the Cattle Rustler

My Aunt Addy came here from Texas in '73. "Too crowded back there," was the way she always put it, and I believed her because even this country started to fill up once the railroad came through.

I have to say, though, that Aunt Addy and Uncle Henry helped the population along, with six kids of their own and me and my sis raised with them. We were kin, taken in when our parents died.

"We'll make do," Aunt Addy said at the time, and that, as I learned, was her motto. Through it all, she "made do."

My sis and I hadn't been at the homestead for more than a few years when Aunt Addy made the first in a series of startling decisions. We were boarding the school teacher that year, Miss Lemon by name, and a falser name nobody ever had. Miss Lemon was as sweet as wild honey, and everybody loved her, especially us kids who fell all over ourselves trying to please her.

As it turned out Uncle Henry lost his head over her, too, right there in the house that was spilling over with his own kids and his wife, although she, like as not, was out on horseback doing his job.

Uncle Henry just wasn't practical. No—what he was, was a fool. He had two homesteads, one in his name and one in his wife's, and a passel of mouths to feed, and what he did was to read and dream and putter around the house and garden, talking to us kids, teaching us our letters and a little bit of history and religion on the side. We loved it, followed him around like chicks, but it was Aunt Addy we went to for advice, or help, or anything practical. It was Aunt Addy who taught us how to make do in the wilderness, where to hide in thunderstorms, how to take a prickly pear and boil it into a poultice for snakebite, and when to plant and harvest. She taught us all to ride and cut calves, too, and to brand them, AH on the left hip. It was Aunt Addy who thought up the idea of sewing silver coins under the skin of her calves' necks. Brands could be changed, she said, but only we knew about those coins. It's a trick that's been used since, but it was her idea at the start.

Anyway, there was Aunt Addy out riding the range, leaving Uncle Henry and the teacher at home to recite poetry and look into each other's eyes, and pretty soon they headed off to the barn and the privacy of the hayloft. But, as I said, Uncle Henry was a fool. He couldn't expect to hide his infatuation from eight kids and a sharp-eyed wife for long, and he didn't.

Aunt Addy came back early one day, her horse having stepped in some cholla, and when she led it into the barn, the first thing she saw was the ruffled petticoat our Miss Lemon was so proud of. Only Miss Lemon wasn't wearing it. She'd left it hanging over the edge of the loft in her haste, and it was there, fluttering like a flag in the breeze.

Aunt Addy went up the ladder quick as a snake and found what she suspected: Uncle Henry in his shirt and shoes and not much else, and Miss Lemon minus her fine lace petticoat. Addy chased the two of them down just as they were, while us kids gaped and sniggered and formulated ideas depending on how old we were and how much we knew at the time.

Aunt Addy followed more slowly, carrying Uncle Henry's pants over her arm. She went across the yard after them and into the house.

What followed was a scene from one of those melodramas, with all of us lined up against the windows and Miss Lemon inside swooning, while Uncle Henry bent over her showing his bare bottom to the sky.

Aunt Addy stood there grim as death, arms folded across her chest. Finally she spoke. "Henry," she said, "get your pants on before your brains get cold."

And when Henry said, "Now, Addy," in that sweet way of his, she said, "Don't 'now Addy' me. You get your pants on and then you get your things, and you and your Miss Lemon here get off my ranch."

Uncle Henry hopped on one foot pulling on his pants. "This here's my home, Addy," he said. He hopped on the other foot.

"No more it isn't," she said. "A man uses his house as a brothel don't have much other use for it." She frowned at Miss Lemon who was sobbing into her handkerchief. "And a teacher who indulges in fornication ain't much of a teacher. You been teaching all my boys or just this one?"

Miss Lemon sobbed harder.

Aunt Addy said, "The two of you are as much use as tits on a mule. Be off my property before sundown. I've had a bellyful of your children. Time you started on someone else."

They left, Miss Lemon leaning on Uncle Henry and carrying her suitcase. Uncle Henry was carrying a trunk full of books. Like I said, he wasn't practical.

We all lined up by the gate to see them go. He shook our hands each in turn, and told us to be good and help our mother. I guess he forgot I wasn't one of his, because he said the same to me and patted me on the head.

Aunt Addy cooked a big pot of beans and ham hocks for supper that night, and opened a jar of piccalilli, and made sour dough biscuits and a dried apple pie, and she sat in

Uncle Henry's place at the head of the old pine table and looked at us. After we'd sopped up the last bean and eaten the pie down to the dish, she gave us our orders.

We were, she said, going to make do. We had our fields of cane and corn, our garden, our beef cattle, our hogs and chickens. We had our backs and our hands and the wits God gave us, and thank God none of us took after Henry. She assigned each of us jobs, the girls getting the kitchen and housework, the boys the hoeing, planting, and herding. We'd sell beeves to the army and to the reservation and the local market. Produce, too, what we could spare. And there was to be no complaining, no shirking, no tomfoolery. And, she added, being as we were near the main road, we'd take in travelers who wanted a bed for the night.

"Rustlers, too?" I asked, for rustlers were what we saw most of, and the posses behind them.

"Rustlers, too," she said, "and nary a word to anyone." She lit up one of Uncle Henry's cigars that he'd left behind in his rush, and we gaped at her in astonishment. "Now this is my place," she said, sitting back and exhaling, "I don't aim to smoke behind the barn." She stared us down and returned to her train of thought. "Rustlers, especially. If we're good to them, they'll leave us alone out of gratitude."

It sounded like good sense to me, though I'd rather have been on horseback than hoeing the fields. The thing about her plan was, she made it sound like an adventure, like something exciting that only grown folks did and into which we were being initiated, and we all rose to the bait as, I'm sure, she knew we would. In our beds that night we whispered about rustlers and outlaws as if a new world had opened up, and in a way it had.

Word about Uncle Henry got round pretty fast because the school had to close and people wanted to know why. Aunt Addy told them, too, straight out. She never did beat about the bush like most women. To those who asked about Henry she said, "He's gone and good riddance. Now

I can stick to business." She did, too. She worked harder than any man I ever saw, not because she was driven to it but because she purely loved it. She told me once she never did feel right except on horseback working cattle or just riding for the pleasure of it.

"It has something to do with freedom," she said, and then she laughed and said me being a boy, I wouldn't understand.

I thought I did, though. Once in awhile I had a day with nothing to do, and I'd go off into the mountains or down onto the flat, and I'd get to feeling wild with all that space to move in. Sometimes I'd take the Mexican pony, Chico, and we'd run just for the fun of it, and no one to tell us to stop. So I thought I pretty well understood Aunt Addy and her love of the outside, of having a good horse under her that knew what she wanted.

Life went on. Uncle Henry's absence didn't change anything much. He'd never been the heart of the place. We all did our share, and willingly, too, because we were happy and didn't want to loose the ranch or be split up or sent away from Aunt Addy.

After awhile, travelers started stopping. All kinds of people: men headed for the silver and copper mines, prospectors searching for gold, families looking for a likely place to settle. We had some Mormons once, and a family of black people, and I can remember staring at that family, never having seen anyone that color.

"Mind your manners, boy," Aunt Addy said to me as I inched closer to see them. She called all of us "boy," because she said she couldn't remember so many names. It didn't signify a lack of affection. We just took it for granted she knew who we were and loved us with or without names.

About the Mormons she had a little more to say. The man had two wives, pretty women, and a bunch of children. "Henry was born to the wrong religion," she said when she saw them. Then she smiled kind of grim. "At least one of them gets a rest once in awhile," she said.

"Maybe there's something in it after all." But she didn't talk much to them because she said down deep she felt bigamy was indecent.

Illegality didn't bother her, however. We put up with plenty of rustlers and enjoyed their company, too. Generally they were nicer and more polite than regular folks. They helped wash up after supper and sometimes they'd tell us kids tales as good as anything in books. Some of them even passed out a coin or two for grooming their horses or making some small repair to their tack.

Black Bob Beaufort was a regular visitor, partly because he had a run between Mexico and the Peak where he branded and hid out his stolen cattle, and partly because he was sweet on Aunt Addy. She was a handsome woman, tall and black haired, and she had a way of moving, quick and sure, that made people look at her.

She had a soft spot for Black Bob, too, because like all strong women she had a weakness for a gentle man. She never could resist one weaker than she was, and with Black Bob she had a prime candidate. She bossed him, bullied him, sometimes even told him how to pull a job. She had the planning kind of mind that he lacked.

"So blamed innocent," she said once. "How a man like that ever came to rustling I can't understand."

However he came to it, Aunt Addy was quick to see its uses.

She was pining for a thoroughbred bull because at that time ranchers were importing all kinds of strains trying to improve their stock. But because there were so many of us, we never had much cash. We ate most of what we produced, and the extra got sold or traded for whatever else we needed. So, though she had her heart set on a good bull, she went without. Until one night on the back porch when she said as much to Black Bob.

Sometimes the two of them would sit there after supper, smoking cigars in the dark and talking about this and that with all of us tucked away somewhere nearby to listen.

That morning Aunt Addy had hid Bob under her bed

when a posse come by looking for him, and she was chuckling over her success and puffing away contented, and then all of a sudden she let out a sigh that would've torn a stronger man than Beaufort in half.

He turned all sweet like he could and moved closer to her. "What's the matter, Addy?" he asked.

She sighed again. Even in the dark I could see the gleam in her eye and was surprised he couldn't. "Nothing," she said.

"Got to be something to make you sigh like that."

"I was just wishing I had me a good bull," she said. She sounded so wistful I had to smile.

"A bull," he said. "What for?"

That was too much for her. "Use your head, man," she snapped. "What do folks usually use bulls for?"

"Oh," he said. And then, "But you got a bull."

"Not a nice Hereford I don't," she said. "Not one like Ike Tyler's got. Everybody's breeding up but me. I've got scrubs. That's all."

He chewed that one over awhile. Then he said, "Addy, I can get you a bull."

"I don't want no stolen animal," she said. "Lying's one thing. Taking a bull with someone else's brand on it's another."

He thought again. I swear I could hear his brains creak. "What if it don't have a brand?" he said.

"That's different. Anybody leaves a good bull out unclaimed don't deserve him."

Black Bob rode out at first light. When he had been gone for four weeks, Aunt Addy got restless.

"I knew it," she said one morning over breakfast. "The dang fool's got himself killed or hanged, and it's my fault. I put him up to it."

"What'd you put him up to?" I asked

"Stealing a bull," she said.

"He does it all the time," I said, trying to comfort her. "That's how he makes a living."

"Lord God," she said. "That don't mean he won't get

caught." She lit a cigar. "I should've gone out and rustled my own."

"Aunt Addy!" I said.

She remembered it was me she was talking to and laughed like she was trying to erase what she'd just said. "I'm joking, boy. You know that."

But I kept thinking of how she'd gone all sad and soft that night on the porch, and I figured she hadn't been joking at all.

That night after supper, Aunt Addy called a conference.

"It's come down to it," she said. "I need a bull and I guess I'll have to work for it. If you all can handle things here, I'm going to town and get work in the saloon."

"The saloon!" we said.

Evie, the oldest, said, "Ma, you can't work in a saloon. It ain't right."

"If I do it, it'll be right," Aunt Addy said.

"I'll go work in the saloon," Evie said, hopefully, I thought.

Aunt Addy gave her a long look from under those straight black eyebrows of hers. "No, Miss, you won't," she said. "You'll stay here and keep yourself decent."

She sighed. "There's another way," she said.

"What?" we asked.

"I can sell Acorn to Ike Tyler."

Acorn was Aunt Addy's cutting mare, and every rancher in the county had his eye on her—six years old, smart and strong, and all over the smooth tan color of an acorn. Working cattle with that mare was a treat. You could close your eyes, sit back, and just hold on. She did the rest.

The thought of trading Acorn for a big, dumb, mean-tempered bull was too much for me. I had another idea. I raised my hand and Aunt Addy looked at me.

"What is it, boy?"

"You oughtn't to sell her," I said. "What you ought to do is, well, you know that big grey stud horse of Ike Tyler's?"

She nodded once, quick.

"You ought to take the mare over there some night. Get you a good colt. Sell the colt and keep the mare. It'll take awhile, but you can always get a bull. Thing is, you'll never get another Acorn."

Her grey eyes narrowed to slits. She thought awhile. Then she said, "Boy, you got sense for such a little bugger. I wish you were one of mine."

I turned red with pleasure. Praise from Aunt Addy was rare.

She said, "You think you can handle that?"

I nodded.

"Good," she said. "We'll keep a check on her. First night she's ready, you'll go."

And I did, in the light of a tracker's moon. I remember that night like it was written in my head; the whip-poor-will crying near the wash, the coyotes singing in the hills, and a flock of ducks flying right across the moon in a world so still I could hear the whistle of their wings.

Something began to ache inside me that night, some hunger I didn't know I had or what it was for, only that I wished nothing would end, that I could stay in that moment forever, with the cottonwood trees white and twisted, the grass blowing like a woman's hair, and the smooth body of the mare moving under me like running water.

I remember it all, even how they looked, mare and stud, bigger than horses, more like two clouds come together in the sky, straining to be together, to pull apart.

When he was done, the stud stood there, slick with sweat and shining as if he was carved out of some white stone. His ears stuck up into the darkness over the heavy curve of his neck, and he whinnied so loud the mountain rang with it all the way home, making the mare quiver between my knees.

After that we waited; for the mare to foal, for Black Bob to come back. Aunt Addy had given up on him, though she didn't say so out loud. She just went on making do.

One morning more than five months after he'd left, Bob came riding up the lane on the sorriest horse I'd ever seen. He was leading a critter that looked like it come straight out of the book of prophecies. White it was, and black spotted, with black circles around its eyes and a hump on its back like a camel. It had a big, floppy brisket that hung nearly to the ground, and a pair of crooked black horns that stuck out above dangling ears.

"What in tarnation is that?" yelled Aunt Addy, completely forgetting her worry.

"I brought you your bull," said Bob. He swung off the horse that stood there heaving, its nose in the dust.

"That ain't no bull," she said. "You made a mistake. That's a spotted clown."

"It's a bull," he said. "Honest. It's a Brahma. I went clear to Texas for him."

"You wasted your time then," she said. "But I am glad to see you back."

He said, "Addy, take a look. It's a bull alright."

She sniffed. "I can see that," she said. "But does he know what he's supposed to do with it?"

Like I said, Aunt Addy always spoke her mind. Not everybody could take her plain speaking, but Beaufort just grinned.

"Yep," he said. "Bet we left spotted calves clear across New Mexico."

"They'll track you down, Beaufort," she said, laughing. "They'll follow them spotted calves right to my door."

"Addy," he said. "I paid for him. Cash. Got him from a circus."

She blinked. "I believe it," she said. "I surely do. Do them spots wash off?"

"This here's an East Indian bull," Bob roared. "He comes by those spots on his own, and he'll stand up to heat and drought better'n any old Hereford or Durham. You believe me, Addy. This here bull will get you good calves."

I looked at Beaufort who'd grown a curly black beard that clung to his gaunt cheeks like mistletoe to a juniper tree. I looked at the horse, skin and bones and not much else. I looked at the bull, fleshed-out, firm, not even in a sweat.

I said, "Aunt Addy, maybe he's right. Look at that critter. He's fresh as dew. Put one of your dimes in him and turn him loose."

She laughed. "Boy," she said, "He don't need a dime. He's got all them spots and a water bag on his back to boot."

But in the end she did all of it, even placed her brand, AH, carefully on his left hip. And she turned him loose, but not before he'd chewed through the vegetable garden and climbed the porch steps to give her a lick with his big tongue.

She ended up having to lead him into the hills where the cows were. "For better or for worse, I got me a trick bull," she said.

For better or for worse, Aunt Addy got a lot of things in the years that followed. In the Spring, Acorn foaled a slate-grey stud colt, even-tempered, playful as a pup, and sound. Aunt Addy couldn't bring herself to part with him.

"Now I've got me a stud and a bull," she said. "I surely do."

And when the cows began to calve, they dropped tough little calves, some spotted, but nary a one with a hump, and they grew and put on weight almost from the air itself.

Black Bob took on a halo in her eyes. "All that time, I thought he was a fool," she said, shaking her head.

Somehow she persuaded him to give up rustling and settle down in our bunkhouse. I don't know what she promised him, but I suspect it was more than regular meals and thirty dollars a month.

Whatever it was, our lives went on, smooth as the passing of seasons. We did what had to be done and took pleasure in it, and pride. There was never time to be bored, but there was always time to look out over the land and fill up with joy, knowing it was ours and that we had, indeed, made do.

Prickly Pear

Cochise County, Arizona, July, 1882. . .

He has gone, leaving his boots at angles on the floor and me in my room with its thick adobe walls, the small window that keeps out heat but lets light enter. I pick up the mirror from the shelf and look at my face, expecting to see sin written there, but I see only a face, darkened by sun, with wrinkles beginning around the eyes. They are not from laughter. I think I have not laughed aloud for years. This afternoon when I smiled at the stranger was the first time I have smiled in years.

My mama wouldn't know this face, nor my girlhood friends in the high-ceilinged houses of Savannah. I have done things never dreamed or spoken of in that life. I have become someone else, perhaps someone more real. Or perhaps not. It could be that my life is no more than the life of a rock on a mountainside, chiseled slowly away by wind and water, scattered, finally, into dust.

No, they would not know me, spare as a yucca stalk, cheek bones high and sharp, black hair I used to curl pulled back into a coil for coolness in the desert heat. Catharine Bascom with her curls and curves, her hoops and dancing feet is gone, and in her place, I am. I, Cat McNeal, who can drive a team of horses, shoot straight as a man and to kill, give birth alone, easily, like a bitch under a table. Cat McNeal, who this afternoon betrayed her husband in this room.

My mama would call me "common" if she could see me, and some vestige of girlhood training that still lingers within me would nod agreement, would fuss over hands, hair, skin in horror at my degradation. But my mama did not make the voyage west by wagon, that journey of hundreds of days, of mud and dust, heat and rain, lack of privacy. My mama and all those other mamas in their sanctuaries would have died of shame at exposing themselves to the prairie grasses under the sky, at coupling in a wagon bed with only a canvas wall between husband and wife and the world.

That was my first lesson. Bodies are there. They receive and are taken, hunger and are torn by birth, disease, mutilation. The world is filled with bodies, and they are all similar. It is the spirit that grows, sings, searches. It is the spirit that leaps at the earth and its distances, at its own image in the face of another; it is the body that must keep up or fail in its duty and be left behind.

It is the space and the emptiness that have wrought these changes in me. I have had to rely on myself for company, advice, aid. I have become mother to myself, deciding the rules, the need for giving or for chastity. I have become my own voice in the wilderness. The alternative was death.

It is earth that has changed me; the prairie that goes on for a thousand miles, the desert dancing in a mirage of light. And here where we have put down our roots and have grown, here in this high valley where the mountains surface just beyond our door, here I have come to know that silence is a necessary thing, surpassing even the need for laughter. I have grown up to meet those monuments of dreadful patience. I have steeled myself to endure.

These last two weeks I have had an abundance of silence. Wells and the four boys, and Jesus the drover have gone into Mexico to deliver some bulls and to bring back calves to fatten. It is the first time that all the boys have gone. They are of an age now to be helpful on the trail, old enough to learn the business of ranching. Rosa, Jesus' wife, was to have been here with me, but her mother is dying, and she went to her weeping, her children around her like a flock of geese.

So I have been alone with only the hounds for company, and the striped cat, and the work mules, and my little mare. I have not been afraid or lonely. There is always the sound of the wind here, and the rush of the creek, full now from the summer rains. And there have been many voices in my head, speaking words, ideas, making a music.

Though I dare not speak of this, there is a peace in being alone, in having the house to myself, empty of husband and sons. No outer voices intrude. Unhurried, I have washed the linen and the clothes and left them to bleach in the sun. Without Rosa, I have cooked what I want, have eaten when I felt the need, often not at the long pine table in the kitchen but out of doors, on the porch, on the flat rock by the creek, and once on the top of the mountain.

That day it took me until almost noon to reach the summit, clambering over rocks, inching along a narrow track where one wrong step meant a long fall, perhaps a slow death with vultures hovering over. Yet I went on. I have always wanted to climb this mountain that overlooks my life, have always wanted to see to the other side.

Up there what I found was more space, the sickle curve of the valley, its grass high and rippling, and mountains rising upon each other's shoulders like tumblers at a carnival.

So many mountains. So much sky. Had I not grown up near the sea, I could believe that land is all there is. I wished I could gather it in my arms, hold it as a mother holds a child, joyous and fearful all at once, for life is brutal, people are harsh. They come, staking claim, tearing up what should be left to dream.

I ate there, high in a meadow of lupine, and when I had finished I scattered the crumbs to the four winds, the only blessing I could give. The wind took my hair. The sun burned my flesh until I felt like spirit only, flayed but stronger for it. I threw back my face to the sky, no longer alien but one who has made a pact with the land. One and the same, we are free, flowing, bearers of fruit, givers of self.

O, I am filled with such heresies, yet in my bones I know they should not be so called. I dare not speak or write them, only keep them alive within, passing them on to no one, for I have no daughters, only sons. I have no way to be heard.

This morning I went out to hoe the corn, high now and tasseled, swaying in the wind. It is hard work, hoeing, digging up weeds that cling to the soil as if they have a right. And they do, for this is their place, those yellow daisies, the twining vetch, the poisonous datura that opens its throat in darkness. Yet I uprooted them all, turned them over, pausing now and then to rest. And when I could work no longer I walked to the creek where the willows bend over and the roots of mesquite twine through the banks. I tucked my skirt at my waist and waded in the clear water. I stood a long time, still as a branch, and dreaming watched water beetles surface and descend, a green frog that hung motionless, suspended like a leaf.

So when the horse plunged its nose in the stream at my feet, it seemed forever before I could move, focus on the rider who sat, reins slack in his fingers. He belonged to the silence, to the dark side, where the shadows are.

Sometimes wolves come down out of the mountains, and cats on padded paws, and when they do I watch them, beasts from a world I cannot penetrate but try to understand. It is so with people, too. We can live with someone, work, love, play, yet remain always outside, locked within our own bodies, denied exit and entrance by the flesh.

But this morning, as frog, green leaf, water, I looked up and saw not only a face but a life like my own gone out of kilter and calling out in despair. Or perhaps I did not see but felt, became that man as I had become my surroundings.

No matter that I stood nearly naked in the water, that my face, my hands were coated with the red dust of the fields. My mama would say that of course it mattered, that I led him on, forgot modesty. And I would answer that modesty is of no use once the spirit has been seen and recognized.

Ah, mama, why did you never speak of this? Why only the warnings, the shame, the pain of hell? Why did you never say that love comes like a gift? Was it fear for me, mama, or did it never happen to you as it happened to me, suddenly, in the middle of a stream? And if I am the only woman ever to have felt, why me, Cat McNeal, with no one to tell, to advise?

I gave myself to him, mama, to that outlaw with the dust of the road on him, and the smells of sweat, whiskey, and fear. I gave myself because he needed but could not ask. Because we were there.

You say that is no reason, but it is the only reason. We cry out in the dark and are heard. We take flight and fall back, and find a hand extended.

He dismounted, took off his hat, held out a hand to me.

"I didn't mean to frighten you, ma'am," he said.

"You didn't." I reached up, came onto the bank, and saw him beaten down by the weight of gun belt and pistols, by sun, heat, years.

He was an outlaw. I'd seen them before. The road to Galeyville is just beyond our fence, and they ride it fast, burdened by stolen money and not much else. They travel light, and there's a look on their faces, a coolness, a dominance. This man had that look, and when he moved, he moved surely, wasting no time, the way a man moves when his life depends on it. I knew he could kill as carelessly as I could hack at a snake. I knew he could, if need be, kill me. Yet there was in his eyes a hollow place, stark as a playa. He stood there, arrogant as God and knowing he wasn't.

Something broke inside me like a germinating seed. I could feel its tendrils spreading, making ready to flower.

Perhaps it was my own isolation that, having found its like-
ness, struggled for recognition, or perhaps it was strength
that had lain unasked for all the years of my life. God and
man had been proved vulnerable. My time had come. I
would gather him up, this image of my own journey. I
would heal our wounds.

"You look like you've traveled a way," I said. "Come up
to the house. I'll give you something to eat."

He smiled. His eyes glittered, and his cheekbones lost
their sharpness. "I don't need food, but I'd like whiskey if
you have any. Women think they can cure everything with
a meal."

"It helps," I said. "But I have whiskey, too. It won't cure
you, either, but it's good whiskey."

"It helps," he said, mimicking me.

"How?"

"It just does. You forget."

"You don't look like you ever forgot a thing," I said.

"Not yet. But I will. One way or another." His eyes
flicked over me, the quick assessment of a foe. People out
here are good at that. One look is sometimes all there's
time for. "Get me that drink" he said.

I said, "I know what you are, and that's your business.
But liquor won't help you stay alive. It'll get you killed
faster."

He snarled at me, lips lifting from his teeth. "Maybe I
want to be killed and have an end to it."

"There's no end to it," I said. "Living's hard. Dying's
worse. Leave your horse here. The grass is good. We'll get
the whiskey."

"I can pay," he said.

"No need. You're welcome to it." I remembered my own
doubts, my decisions made alone. "You want to tell me anything, you can," I said. "It's good talking sometimes. Out
here especially."

He came close, bent down. I could see red veins in his
eyes, the dust in the lines of his face. He smelled from old
liquor, older fears.

"I killed the first because I had to. Because my family expected it. And then I killed again. It got easy. And now they're coming, the coyotes, the vultures, the trash I wouldn't have spoken to before. The snot-nosed kids wanting to grow up fast, and the old ones gone soft and hoping to retire by killing me. They come and they come, and Christ, even in my sleep they're there, and when I ride out they're behind the rocks on their bellies like snakes." He waved his hand at the empty road.

"I write letters home and lie. I don't tell them I'm a killer. A wanted man. How can I say it? And they write back and say, 'Come home. Settle down.' They say they love me, but they don't know what it means, what they mean. Life is a goddamned lie." He shook his head at me. "You know that? You in your pond with your hair down, sweet as a pear . . . life is a lie?"

"I'm a woman," I said. "I was raised in a lie. I wasn't supposed to be real. I wasn't supposed to know what people really need."

He was listening, head to one side. I thought that no one had touched him for a long time. And no one had needed me. I put my hands on his chest. "I was raised not to ask questions, just do what I was told. And then I came out here, and just to stay alive, I had to change. Out here there's no one to tell you. You know that. And you know you'd not just stand and let some fool gun you down. You do what you have to."

He looked as if he hadn't heard or didn't understand. I took a breath. "When we first came, I killed a man," I said.

He stared at me. "You?" he said. "You?"

"Me." I laughed, but it came out harsh. "Me. Sweet as a pear. A prickly pear, more like. I was alone with the baby. An Indian came after me in the house, and I shot him. Buried him. And I'd do it again. You do what's needed. And you don't go back or go home. You can't. Because no matter what they say, that place isn't there for you anymore."

He didn't believe me. Like a man he carried an ideal in his head and ran blindly in search of it.

"Let's go on up," I said. "You can have your whiskey and a wash, too."

We went through the back pasture, through the tall grass, the gaillardias, the yellow daisies. The house stood at the top, four-square, with thick adobe walls, slanted tin roof, a porch running around it for shade. One of the hounds lay there panting. He raised his head, saw me, lay back again with a sigh. The wind had dropped. It would rain soon.

"Your place?" he asked.

I nodded. "Mine and my husband's." I put out my hand as I saw his shoulders go tense. "It's alright," I said, soft, easy like I talked to my mare. "I'm alone. They're all trailing calves in Mexico."

He said, "You're a fool."

"You'd find out soon enough." I smiled then. "I've told you everything else."

"You haven't told me your name," he said.

I didn't want to tell. My name was all I had left. "Catharine," I said.

"Catharine . . . Cat . . . I need that drink," he said.

The first drops of rain spattered in the dust. "Come on then." We ran but he stopped at the door, scenting the air for danger where there was none, where there was only me coiling my hair back into its knot.

"Leave it be," he said. He came in, stood looking down, pulling my hands away and putting his big hard ones around my skull.

I let him have his way. The touching had to be. Words go. The fingers remember, and the long muscles of the body. The rain came hard, slamming the door, intruding itself between earth and sun and shrieking in its own night. Hailstones hit the roof like gunfire, ran rattling down into the gutters. No one will come, I thought. No one.

I said, "Take off your guns. No one's coming," and went to get a bottle of the whiskey Jesus makes in his still up the wash.

He sat down, closed his eyes, opened them when I put the whiskey on the table.

"Don't you remember what it was like?" he asked. "Don't you care? A woman like you doesn't belong in the fields. A woman like you shouldn't have to kill a man. You shouldn't even know what it feels like to want to." He sucked at the liquor.

"You talk like my mama," I said. I laughed again at the irony of the world conspiring in a vision of me that had no place in life. "You still believe in the old lies. I don't. What you want and what you get aren't ever the same."

"Better dead then," he said. He leaned forward and put his face between my breasts. I felt his breath sharp as a knife where the buttons of my dress opened. I smelled his sweat, familiar as my own. I felt I had come home to an old nest.

"Not death," I said. "Not yet."

"It's what's left."

I held him as I would have held the earth. "We're left."

"Why me?" he said. "Why now?"

"You're here now."

"Why couldn't it have been before? We'd have gone home."

I said, "Because it couldn't, that's all. And home isn't a place. It's people like you and me for this little time."

"Dying is going home," he said. He pushed me away.

I stamped my bare foot hard on the floor. "Go ahead, then," I said. "Go out and die if that's what you want." I wept for my wanting, his refusal.

"Christ," he said. "Don't cry."

"I will. I'll cry as much as I please. For you with your guns and your whiskey and your running away."

He went cold as stone. "I never run away." He stood up, shook me like a rag. "If you were a man, I'd kill you."

"Go ahead," I said. "Kill me. Then run off. That's what you all do. Keep on moving. Keep on looking for what you've got right in your hands."

I could not bear to let him go and me naked without him. I pulled his head down, kissed him, heard the sound he made.

We were not gentle in our joining. We fought and lashed out, not at each other but at death that waited, howling like the wind outside. And I thought I had won when the thrusting stopped and we lay wrapped in separate but similar peace.

He said, "Cat . . . Catty . . ."

"Go to sleep. I'll watch," I said, smiling. I would love and love again to keep death away.

The storm passed over. The sun found the window and cut through while I watched. But even in his sleep he heard the hooves before I did and sat upright, taut as a line.

"Stay here," I said. "I'll see who it is."

"Tell them you haven't seen me," he said. "Tell them you've been here all day. But for Christ's sake, don't tell them you're alone."

I fastened my skirt, buttoned my blouse. Harlot, I thought. Temptress. I had loved a man whose name I did not know. I said, "I don't even know who you are."

"Better," he said. He pulled on his belt and some cartridges spilled onto the floor. "That way, if they ask have you seen me, you can't say."

"You think I'll never call out for you," I said. "But I will. Even without a name."

"You forget me," he said. "You keep safe, hear?"

I nodded, knowing there was no forgetting. I had found him and lost, and I would pay the price. "You stay alive," I said.

There was a pounding on the door. "I'll be back," I said, and ran, coiling my hair.

The man on the porch was like the one within—lean, quick, deadly. Only with him there was no leap into unity, no sudden insight into despair. Enemy he was. Killer.

I went out, closing the door behind me.

He tipped his hat. "Sorry to bother you, ma'am," he said. "I'm looking for a friend who was riding this way. We got split up in the storm."

I looked into his eyes, hard and blue like pieces of shale. I said, "I was out yonder. I didn't see anybody."

He frowned. "Can I look in your barn?"

"Go ahead," I said. "Just watch out for that brown mule. He doesn't take to strangers."

I heard the creak of a porch board around on the other side, and I moved to cover the noise.

"Water your horse at the trough," I said, hoping to give him time to reach the creek. "Who is it you're looking for anyway?" I thought I was clever, asking that. I thought I could possess him, given his name.

"John Ringo," he said. "You know him?"

I shook my head. "No." But my body chanted at me, "Lies, lies."

I said, "You help yourself at the well. The water's good." And I came in to hide the bottle, wash the glass, to look at my face that is still the same . . .

He has left his boots. How far can he go without boots on this land with its cactus, insects, slicing stones? And how do I account to Wells for them, black calfskin and sized for a man? Or for the cartridges on the floor? I gather them all in my apron, go down to the creek where the horse still grazes and leave them there near the willow. I throw the cartridges into the water. They gleam, sink, and are gone. No trace now. Only the warmth in my belly. I have not made the bed. Tonight I will lie in it alone and call . . .

I sit on the porch, a pan of cold beans in my lap. I have been sitting here all afternoon, eating idly, wondering why we pass our lives in the company of strangers. I have milked the cow, put the milk in the well. I stare out to the mountains. The land glows orange in the sunset. Rocks catch fire. The field leans in the wind like a flame.

Swifts fill the sky, rising, gliding, falling away silver and singing. I understand them now. I know what bodies can do. I will sleep here on the porch. He must come back for his boots, his horse. He cannot go without them. If he passes, I will hear. I will call his name . . .

They say it was suicide. They say he came to the old oak with its five black branches, shot himself and died, alone, bootless. They say these things over and over, but I do not believe any of it. They say he is buried on the bank beneath stones from the creek bed. That he sleeps now, at peace. I do not believe in peace. Not for him. Not for me. I believe only in endurance. So I do not go there. I do not want to see the grave or the tree or his brains spattered on the bark.

I will never go there. When I ride out I will turn my mare's head toward the mountains. And I will hope their silence comforts me.

Sunflower

No one seeing Clay and me now—Clay sitting on the rusted chair under the live oak, the spectacles he got at the dime store slipping down his nose because, whatever he says, I know he's taking a nap and not reading the Bible, and me, gone grey-headed like the seed pod of a sunflower and small-breasted to boot—no one would think I was young once and so foolish I near ruined my marriage and myself.

They mightn't even think I paid the price for what I did, seeing Clay and me, contented, in a decent house, curtains at the windows, my flowers and my yellow cat by the door. They'd be wrong, though. The Bible tells us, "As ye sow, so shall ye reap," and it's true. Not that life's been all bad or all that hard to take, but I figure there could have been a bit more joy in it, the kind of light-weight feeling I used to have, just fit to bursting with excitement and romance. The way I felt when I was young and yellow-haired, and every man for fifty miles was courting me, lining up on the front porch, evenings, or crowding round to dance on a Saturday night at the fairgrounds, and stealing a kiss or two in the shadows by the corrals. Maybe, though, feelings like that belong only to the young, have no place when you're sobered up and married. I don't know. I never spoke about it to anyone, not even Clay. Never to Clay. He's been good to me, better than I deserve, but I never felt I could ask him where the joy went, the mystery, the never knowing what's going to happen, only that it's going to be so wonderful you're not sure you can stand it. He might have thrown it up to me, and I don't think I could've stood that.

I used to wake up happy every morning back then, and run to the window to see what kind of day it promised to be, and then to the old mirror where I'd stand and brush my hair and shake it loose like silk. Then back to the window to see if Miguel had left his scarf tied round the corral post. If he had, it meant I'd find him somewhere, and we'd go off, not for long because he was supposed to be working. But we'd find time for kisses down by the wash, and we'd talk a bit and, later on, we got more serious, touching, lying together under an old tree whose branches came down all the way to the ground and made a kind of tent.

My Ma and Pa never knew about those meetings. Or my sisters or brothers, either. No one ever found out, even after I'd married Clay. After I knew I'd made a mistake and tried to change it.

It was just that I was young and didn't know much about folks or about love, either. What Miguel and I did down by the wash had nothing to do with living. It had nothing to do with the way my parents acted together, or with the way any grown folks acted, all tight and tired and full of do's and dont's. What we did was wild and sweet as the flowers we crushed under us, as the branches moving overhead, and now and again a bird singing as if we weren't even there, or as if we belonged. What we did didn't need words, though Miguel had plenty in two languages, and he called me every pretty name he knew and made promises I believed in. We'd have us a ranch someday, over the border in Mexico, and we'd be rich, and I'd wear ruffled dresses, and all the men would tremble at the sight of my yellow hair, my blue eyes, my breasts firm and ripe as apples. And

I'd lie there with my arms around him, my face in his hair, believing it all.

One day, though, my Pa called me in and told me to choose. Just that. "Choose," he said, "and let the county go on about its business." And clear the way for my young sisters, raring at my heels.

And I swear I never thought choosing would end it. I don't know why. I guess I was just plain dumb. Dreamstruck. I thought life would go on easy, and me sucking the sweetness out like a bee.

So I chose. I looked them over, all those men, rich and poor, smart and some dumber even than I was, and I thought of Clay Eddy who didn't come around much but who had a way of looking at me out of his grey eyes that made me shiver when I remembered it. Clay who never talked much, but who told me once I had a laugh like water in a creek, and if he had a thirst he'd walk ten miles to get to me.

The Eddys were a big family, and well off. There's been Eddys here since the early days, always will be. But none of ours. Not even a yellow-haired daughter from the two of us. We were mismatched from the start.

Clay's father gave us a section up in the foothills as a wedding present, and Clay, well, he was set on moving there as soon as possible. "We got to have our own place," he kept saying. "Our own place" those first months was a lean-to out in a pasture. We were ten miles from our neighbors and years away from town, from laughter, dancing, and Miguel.

I was a married woman off in the high country with a man I didn't really know. A man who was mainly silent and thinking, who didn't dance and had no time for company. He was building "our place." I cooked over an open fire in that lean-to, and bedded down at night on an old mattress he'd drug up in the wagon, and I remembered how Miguel and I had lain in the grass and laughed and touched and never worried if we knew each other or not.

At night sometimes, Clay would sit out front looking at

the stars and naming them. He'd say, "Come out and sit, Susannah," and I'd go out for a spell, and he'd tell me about the stars and the planets, about things I didn't understand and didn't care about. I wanted to dance. I wanted to go down on a Saturday night and be twirled around by my husband, followed by the men I'd spurned, envied by the girls. I wanted him to tell me about my laugh, about my hair, about how he was building a ranch to make us rich and buy me things. And all he ever talked about those nights was stars and history.

I felt like the girl I was had died and been resurrected into a woman I didn't recognize and couldn't get the shape of. Worse, that seemed to be what everyone expected. No one thought it was hard on me, going off with my husband. They made jokes and laughed and teased, and told me how lucky I was and how clever to have married an Eddy, to have caught Clay, the hardest working of them all.

I guess that saved him though. When I disappointed him he threw himself into whatever he was doing to forget. And I disappointed him from the start. I could never be easy with him, not in talk or in bed. A man has rights once he's married. I knew that. But I couldn't relax with him, and after awhile he took to watching me as if he expected to find out something, as if he were puzzled and looking for an answer.

"I wish you'd quit watching me," I said one day.

He blew out smoke from his cigarette and stared at me. "I never heard it was wrong, takin' pleasure looking at your wife," he said.

"It just makes me jumpy," I said. "Like I did wrong."

"Did you?"

I turned on him, quick as a deer. "No," I shouted. "No."

"Well then," he said, "you got no reason to worry."

He went outside to watch his stars and didn't come in till after I'd gone to bed. And he didn't wake me like he did sometimes, calling, "Suze," low in my ear, his hand on my breast. Not that night or the next. But then he came in carrying the biggest bunch of wildflowers I ever saw. He knew

I loved flowers, and he stuck them in a jug on the table and said he'd been thinking we should take the wagon and go see my folks and then stop awhile in town.

I thought of Miguel, and hugged him tight around his waist. He closed his eyes and said, "Suze, Suze," and took his way with me right there.

By September we had two rooms built and roofed over with tin. And there was space to expand, "When the time comes," Clay said. He was thinking of sons. Everyone was, my folks and his. Everyone but me. I kept thinking about winter. About being snowed in and no way out and nothing to do but sew on the new machine Clay bought me or look out at the junipers covered up, bent down with ice. And every time I thought about it, I'd panic like an animal in a trap because I had no place else to go.

When I said I'd like to spend a month down in the valley, Clay looked at me. His eyes had shadows in them, as if I'd hit him and it hurt, but all he said was, "You'll like it up here, Suze. Give it a chance. You've never seen these mountains in the snow. Or listened to 'em." One side of his mouth curved up. "You got to learn to be easy. To take what comes and go with it. Stop fighting the bridle."

"And you got to stop talking to me like I'm one of your horses," I said. "I don't like it here all quiet with nothing to do but work in the garden or pedal that machine. No people, no fun, no nothing day in and day out. Why should I sew anyway? Who ever sees me?"

"I'm here," he said. "Or don't I count?"

It went on like that, peaceable for days, and then we'd start cutting at each other with sharp little words and then with no words at all until I thought I'd scream just to smash the quiet.

I spent weeks canning vegetables, filling the shelves with food for the winter, putting pork down in brine and curing bacon. I did it all because I'd been raised to it, not because I was proud, or set a good table, or wanted to please. I did it because it was harvest, and because, if I hadn't, I'd have gone mad.

In September Clay went off on a roundup and left me alone. I cried, walked the floor, chewed my fingernails down till they bled, and I thought of taking the mule and running off, but as I said, I had no place to go. My folks would've sent me back as fast as I'd gone. Then, toward sunset one evening, Miguel came up on his big paint horse. He knew Clay was gone, and he took the chance. When I saw him I bawled like a calf and brought him inside, and learned what it was I'd given away so easily. What I could never get back.

That winter war was declared. There was fighting in places I'd never heard of and couldn't imagine. Clay bought us a radio, ran it off batteries he powered with the windmill. We didn't have electric here till years later, we're that isolated. But all winter I sat and listened to that radio, music mostly, and the love stories, and when Clay wasn't around I sang some and danced, and made believe Miguel was there with me. Because Clay, when he came in, he had to have the news, had to get his old books off the shelf and look up all those places with their funny names. He'd get to talking about wars and generals, armies and back history till I thought I'd scream.

One night I did scream, I was just so tired of hearing about the Japanese and the Germans. "Whyn't you go enlist, you're so fascinated?" I yelled.

"You'd dance plenty, then," he said. "I can see it all. You making fools of us both." He clicked off the radio, put his books back neat the way he did everything.

"Come Spring, you go down to your folks," he said. "I've signed on as foreman at Howson's. We're going to be busy selling beeves to the army. Maybe when I'm done, you'll have growed up a bit."

After that he slept in the barn with Ringer the mule. I remember hoping he'd freeze in there. I remember thinking he cared more for that mule than for me, and I didn't know whether to be glad of it or cry.

So I went home and found everybody too busy to worry about whether I was happy or not. It was Spring, the prettiest time. The cactus were blooming and the yuccas were in bud, and the washes were all running with the thaw. Everywhere I looked I saw critters making nests or giving birth. Even my own sister who'd caught a husband right after me, was swelling up with child.

I started meeting Miguel under the tree, going back to dreaming like I'd never left. I was Susannah again, and I had a dark, quick-fingered man who loved me, called me his angel, put the magic back into me.

But nothing ever lasts. Not happiness, anyway. Not that feeling like you're all in one piece and proud of it. I was like one of those cactus plants that bloom for a night, throwing all their sweetness into a tiny space and then withering on the stem.

The army caught up with Miguel. He couldn't prove he had any need to stay where he was, not with ten other cowboys to do his job. Besides, he was Mexican. Nobody cares about them. I was the only one, and his mother, down on the border with a bunch of other children.

I cared so much I went off to town the day before he left. We took a room in the hotel where the salesmen stay, and the cattle buyers. We had one night, using the bed for what it was made for, over and over, and me crying like a young 'un and holding on like I was fighting off the whole U.S. government and the President thrown in to boot. I went to the station, too. I hurt so bad I didn't care who saw me, who would go running to Clay with the tale. I couldn't imagine any life after I watched that train ease out through the mesquite and the scrub toward the mountains and the sea.

I stood there a long time, till I couldn't see anything but its dust, and when I turned around, it was like I wasn't anybody at all. I never saw the man till I walked right into him, and then what I saw was the watch chain across his stomach, heaving and shining. Even today all I remember about him is that watch chain and his eyes, flat like dimes and colorless, with nothing behind them so he looked blind.

"Whoa, there, Miss," he said. "Everything alright?"

"No," I said. I backed off, tried to go around him.

He figured it out pretty quick. "Your husband, huh? Too bad. Too bad." Those window glass eyes of his flashed at me.

"Leave me be," I said. "Just leave me be."

"That's just what I won't do," he said. "You go walking out on the street like that, you'll get killed. I'll walk along with you." He took my arm and somehow moved me out to the street.

"Now," he said. "You got someplace to go?"

I had never had anyplace to go. I shook my head.

"Now look, Miss," he said. "You got someone waiting? You can't just stand here in the street."

"The hotel," I said. "I'll get there."

"You will and that's a fact because that's where I'm going." He started walking fast, his hand under my elbow. I didn't say anything. There didn't seem to be words to get rid of him. I didn't protest either when he steered me into the hotel bar. It was dark in there and cool. I leaned my head back against the leather seat.

"You need a drink" he said. "What'll you have?"

I said, "Lemonade."

That made him laugh. I remember that, him laughing so loud people turned to look.

He brought me a glass that had ice in it, and a red cherry, and a slice of orange.

"You drink that," he said. "That's more like it."

And I did, tasting it carefully first like a horse testing water. It was good, that drink. I gulped it down, sweet and sour and cold, ate the orange and the cherry. He brought me another.

After awhile, even those wall eyes of his didn't bother me, or the fact that, under the table, his hand moved up my leg clear to the top.

Nothing seemed to matter. Looking back, I sometimes wonder what does matter. Whether what people do on this earth makes a speck of difference. If I'd just settled down in the mountains with Clay and never gone off to that hotel,

would that have made my days different? Or Clay's? I
somehow doubt it. People throw their time of grace away
one way or another, without stopping to think that maybe
that's the happiest they'll ever be.

Mornings now, I don't get up and run to the window, or
to look in the mirror. Certainly there's nothing I'll see in the
glass will make me feel better. Scrawny, with a gap in my
side teeth where the wall-eyed man hit me. The other places
don't show. I'm the only one knows they're there, except
Clay, and he's been trying to forget as long as I have.

I don't remember all of what happened. Don't want to.
He got me drunk. Me, the dumb girl from the mountain,
who'd never tasted hard liquor in her life and didn't know
what it could do taken on top of grief and a sleepless night.

He got me upstairs to that little room I'd been in with
Miguel. When he started pulling at me, I fought back, I remember that much. That's when he hit me, hard, across
the face so my teeth cracked and my nose started to bleed.

He called me names, too, and said some awful words,
and I tried to scream. He held me down on the floor, one
big hand across my throat so I could hardly breathe. I spattered blood across his shirt front where that watch chain
was. That's what I see. That and those weird, flat eyes like
stones, and the man part of him pushing out of his trousers
ugly and red and made for hurting, for coming at me until
something cracked in my head and I couldn't feel or see
anything at all.

Thing is, nobody knew who he was, and I was in no
shape to give any description. I lay on that floor till the next
day when the girl came in to make the bed and found me.
Then I lay in the hospital like I was dead for a week. Every
time I woke up I'd start screaming, so they had to give me
things to keep me asleep. I remember my Ma's face, her
mouth in a straight line like it used to get when she was
mad, and her eyes all red like she'd been crying. Clay was
there, too, in his city suit, sitting beside the bed. I started
screaming when I saw him. I was afraid he'd come at me

with those cold words of his, afraid of what he'd say, what he'd call me. The wall-eyed man's words were still loud in my head, crazy-sounding.

But Clay was always there. Whenever I'd open my eyes, I'd see him, hands between his knees, edgy, the way he gets when he's in the house too long.

Finally I said, "Don't you have anything to do but sit there watching me?" It was horrible to say that, and him faithful as a hound all that time, but I figured I'd get it over with.

He said, "You feel better?"

"No," I said.

"Your Ma's been in every day. She's staying at your Aunt Fran's."

"Where've you been?"

"Here," he said.

I thought about that. I couldn't fathom it, him staying there with me. "What for?" I asked.

"I had to see you were alright."

I started to cry. "Alright," I said. "I'll never be alright. And you got no reason to stay here. Not now."

"You're my wife, Suze," he said. "Don't you know what that means?"

I didn't. I never had. Truth was, I'd never thought about much besides myself.

"You can divorce me," I said. "You got reason."

He bent over the bed and looked at me. I think I'll always remember how he took a piece of my hair and looked at it like he'd never seen it before.

"What happened was a fool thing," he said. "And I'm not blaming you. Maybe it's part my fault, too, for leaving you alone." He spread my hair out over his hand. "I came to take you home, but maybe that's a fool thing, too. I thought I'd get you well up on the mountains, but you can't stand it there, can you? Not it. Not me."

I'd stood him well enough before we were married. I thought about that. About the silence between us, high as a wall.

"You used to talk so pretty," I said. "Now you just talk about things I don't care about. Things I don't understand. And then you come at me like you don't care, just because you've got the right."

His mouth slanted up on one side in that way he has of laughing at the world. "I care," he said, "but a man can't change his nature."

"And I can't change mine."

"Is that it, then?" he said.

I didn't know. I hurt, inside and out. I had nowhere to go, no one except him to care for me, and every thought I had and tried to follow whirled away like flood water, muddy and quick. The thing was, I didn't have any other life. I'd been a daughter, then a wife, with only a few hours of something else between. Something that glittered and was gone, fool's gold, mirage. But Clay was there, steady as those stars of his. "I care," he'd said.

"I'll come home." I closed my eyes so I wouldn't see the brightness on his face. It was something that didn't belong to me.

He put his hands on my shoulders, easy, and then around my face. "If you don't like it there, we can go someplace else," he said, close to my ear.

He was too close. I needed a longer time. I kept my eyes closed. "It'll do fine," I said.

A week later, we went home.

Miguel got killed in the second year of the war on an island in an ocean I've never seen but have to believe is there because everyone says it is.

And Clay and I have just stayed here on the mountain doing like folks have always done, working to feed ourselves and put a little by.

Clay put in a flower garden for me that first year after I came back. It's running a bit wild now, but it's got some of the prettiest flowers—lilies and oxalis, and a bush of yellow roses that the bees just love. And I've got me a hedge of sunflowers, as tall as the house with bright, raggedy petals that wave in the wind all summer, and seeds I save for the winter birds. There's my white leghorns, too, that lay eggs like no hens I ever saw. They're so purely white they hurt my eyes sometimes when I see them in the sun.

I've even learned a bit about the stars. Not much be-cause it's the sunsets I love, all those colors swirling around the mountain. Red, orange, yellow like my lilies open to bursting. Some evenings Clay watches with me, and then I sit with him and wait for the stars. It's pleasant, resting on the porch knowing those stars will be there no matter what.

And the happiness? Well, maybe we're each given a little piece and that's all. Or maybe this here, me and this old man who took me back and never said a word against me, who never forced me or laid a hand on me till one day I was ready, who kept me decent and bought me what he could to give me pleasure, maybe this here is enough.

Part II. Mesa Country

Now. . .

Mesa Country

We are here in the house that looks Westward toward mesa country with its striations of blue, red, lavender, with its mingling of earth and sky, and we are angry, we confront one another, glowering like enraged bulls. It is an anger akin to lust, and we swell with it; he would like to shake me until my neck snaps like a stem. I would like to throttle him, putting my hands around his throat until he croaks for mercy, pleads forgiveness for what he has or has not done. I am not sure who did what, who started this argument. Nor do I care.

What I care about is that we are here, in the house that we dreamed for years, and that we are threatening the nest, endangering our selves and our desires. We have achieved; now we perceive the shadows and must thrash out places, duties, reasons for our selves.

"That's you," he yells. "Just like all women."

Nothing makes me angrier than when he compares me to the females heretofore in his life. It is demeaning, unfair. It makes of me a schemer, a spider, a sexpot, using my body as lure instead of the way I think I use it—as a vessel to receive him. He is a magnificent lover. My delight, my stirrings, like a seed coming to light, tell me this.

"Men think because they lust that women want them to. That they make them do it. You don't know anything about how I feel. How you feel. You're a man."

"Goddamn right!" He is standing there straight and tall, like a tree. Like a man. He is beautiful when he is angry, his face composed of lines and angles; dark brows, mustache, white teeth. If I were an artist I would paint him like this— hawk darting for the kill. But I am not a painter. He is. I paint with words.

"Goddamn right!" he repeats. "And you don't own me."

"Who in hell wants to? Nobody owns anybody else. That's just more of your mixed-up conception of women. You don't own me, either."

He snorts. His black hair falls over his forehead. Blue-beard. Black Jack the pirate. Unapproachable, furious male. "It's all you want. To keep a man. To own his soul."

"I don't want your soul. I've got one. And what about me? You own my body. Do you see me giving it to anybody else? Do you hear me complaining?"

"You do and you can kiss me goodbye. I learn fast."

"If you think I ever would!" How can he think it? Say it? "You should know better than that."

"I do." His face softens. We stare at one another's mouths, those instruments of words, of hurt and pleasure. I am sick of all but the pleasure.

But why am I turning pliable? Why must I be the one to rush in, touch, stroke, twine about him, man, tree? Let him stand there fighting his urges. Let him see who is enslaved by the body.

I go to the window. It is a small room, and he is a big man, bigger in anger. The afternoon stretches West. One behind the other, mesas rise and seem to float, neither earth nor sky. They are both dream and the reality behind the dream, luminous, shimmering, yet solid to the touch. The bones of earth, from here they appear as spirit, mysti-cal as flight. I could fly if I leaned out toward them, if I spread my arms and, running, jumped. They tug at me, lure me. My breath comes out in a whisper. "Yes . . ."

When I turn back he is goaded to further anger by what appears to be rebuff. "Look. Look there," I tell him so he will share the soaring with me. He must. It is all a part. The flight. The scream. The coming to earth. Oh, why does he stare at me? Why do I respond, opening my arms, my mouth like a flower to his tongue the bee, buzzing, darting, sipping? Does he not know I am helpless, hopeless in it?

No. He has his own anguish to deal with. It is all he sees. He is as drugged by my mouth as I am by his. We are equally infirm, equally unable to admit infirmity.

"We could put the bed here," he says. "You can look at them while we make love."

Oh, Man, will that give me pleasure? To look at them instead of you, to focus on illusion when reality is upon me? "No. They'd distract," I say, holding the back of his head, pulling to me while he laughs.

"Let's stop arguing," he says, against me.

I agree. For so long we have had this dream. It is a dangerous place to be, the core of fantasy. As dangerous in its way as for him to be entrapped by the vessel that is my self, that accepts, closes round him, and fears its shattering as much as he fears losing his way in the dark and shifting country of my heart.

In the morning when we wake, the mesas hover beyond the window. I could put my hand out, lift them up, learn them—rock, pebble, glint of ore, beads of sky. Instead I touch his hip, so different from my own. I watch his face, a proud man's face even in sleep.

"I'm responsible for you," he says, suddenly.

And I, always flare to his match, respond, "No! You are not. I am. We have only ourselves."

A ray of sunlight strikes his eyes. His pupils contract to nothing. The irises, clear amber, dazzle. "Do you have to be so opposite?" he asks.

"Yes. Because I am."

Foolish argument. Possessor or possessed, we are bound up, threaded together, warp and woof, male and female, the landscape of our souls, our bones, as infinite, as varied as what I see from the window. It changes with shadows, with light, yet cannot, does not change.

Ensnared, he beats his wings, lifts his head, looks out. "I'm going to town," he says.

I stand at the door, arm high, the old gesture, the eternal female blessing. Vaya con Dios. Hurry home. Come back safe.

It is we who are left on doorsteps, at airports, bus stations. We who know the meaning of the act, the blessing inherent in it. To work, to war, to conquer the earth they go, and we remain, clutching our fears, our hope.

Possessed, I yearn after his dust, I turn, enter the kitchen, sit, coffee in hand looking after, looking out of self to self.

And he. What does he think on the curving road? Does he imagine possible betrayal, disappearance? Does he trust? Or none of these? Perhaps it is the road that is important to him now, the lifeline to the world of men, of action, an unfurling statement of independence.

Oh, who knows what is in the mind and heart of another, even in moments of love?

Once I asked him, "How does it feel for you?"

And he said, "A tingling, a warmth, and then the dark bursts open."

What we endure for it, the moment of brilliance. What we must overcome. Old wounds, the fierce, unending drive for self-protection, the knives of words. Yet we have done it. We have fought doubt, terror, reached out helpless for the other, for the self, hungry in the caverns of our bodies, our hearts.

I wash the dishes, straighten the bed, shake sand from the rugs. I stand out of myself watching, smiling a supercilious smile at this persona who scurries, labors, is precise in her tasks, who cannot help herself in this or any other urge but must clean and decorate her place of rest.

Here is the lure, more surely than the body. The house, the safety of walls, of arms wrapped around protecting the dark place.

This is not meant any more than the other is meant. It is a ritual performed in solitude, a dance, a prayer, an instinctive superstition. Cook! Clean! Prepare! Bathe in scented water and light the lamp, and he will come. He will find his way back though the road be treacherous, the night long.

The mesas stretch themselves. The flowers turn, follow the sun in its passing. Little fears combine into yearning, a quiver of loneliness, pain. "Come home. Come home."

I go out, stand on the dry earth shading my eyes to see the length of the long road out. Another unlearned gesture repeated in multiplicities of yards and doorways, roads and fields. Old. Old as bodies and desire, as the dance of my heart at his approach.

He comes, grim-faced, doubtful, hesitant of our truth. I hold my arms wide and welcome him in.

We live in tumult. Everyone. No flight over the mesas, only the tortured crawling. Up. Rest. Down. Begin again. It is the resting place we yearn for, strive to keep. It is the constant dream achieved, lost, found again. It is the leap of mesas into sky, the stretch of prairie in blue evening. It is man and woman divided, separate, coming together; a collision mellowed by sweetness, by our need for that sweetness. Then fueled for the journey we continue. Up. Down. Rest again, and oh, how we stretch out our arms. How we hurry to the place of dreams.

Blood Ties

They'd be coming in a few minutes—Fern and Tom and the grandkids, Tom easing the sedan over the ruts like the city boy he was, and Fern hanging out the window watching the stony edge and shouting directions, while the twins bounced in the back seat in anticipation of a country visit.

Emma wished they wouldn't bother making the trip. She hated eating in restaurants with their crowded rooms and indifferent meals, hated most of all having to listen to her children's repetitious coaxing.

"It's so far out, Ma. Anything could happen to you. Look what happened to Leanne."

Emma knew what had happened. Leanne had died, alone and unattended, and she, Emma, had found her, tiny as a leaf in the big brass bed and looking pleased with herself, as if even in death she'd managed the unexpected. The thought of dying didn't bother her so much as the thought of dying locked in a small room surrounded by the faces of strangers.

"We've got a spare room and bath. You'd have your privacy." Tom was more sensitive than Fern, more like Emma than any of her children.

"I'll think about it," she'd tell them, waving them off from behind her front gate with a sense of relief. "But I'm not near dead yet."

Then she'd stand watching their car move slowly down the road. By the time it reached the big gate in the pasture fence, all that she could see was the dust stirred up by its passing, and the silence would be back as if it had never been disturbed by voices or the roar of the engine.

She knew she'd never be able to explain that what she loved most of all was the silence. She fed on it. It soothed her as nothing ever had. She didn't need conveniences or the caperings of grandchildren she hardly knew for amusement. What she wanted was what she had; a house with a porch where she could sit and watch the moon rise, the deer browsing among the mesquite, the hawks painting the sky; where no effort or fancy speech was required of her, only the ability to see, absorb the peace, and think.

It had been a lifetime coming, this solitude, and she savored every minute of it. It was hers as nothing else had been; not Nick whom she'd married at seventeen, nor their children, four of them, and none planned or even especially welcomed.

Times had been hard back then; the cattle market shot to hell by the weather and the Depression, the drought drying the range to the color and texture of straw. Through it all she worked as hard as a man, maybe harder, for hers had been the double task of motherhood and ranch hand. But it left her with little time for individual nurturing. Before she realized it, her children were formed, were people and strangers as much as people in town were strangers.

What kept her going were moments when the land revealed itself to her; slices of such piercing clarity of vision that she would stop, breathless, and let the beauty wash over her: the jeweled streaming of migrating Monarch butterflies, the curve of a leaf, coyotes howling, their voices slivers of moon.

She would clasp her hands at her breasts and stare, and the life at her feet would be blotted out, but never for long enough.

"Your Ma's having one of her spells," Nick used to say to the kids, his voice edging toward laughter. A tender laughter, true, but unfeeling, or so it seemed to her, torn between two realities.

More often than not she'd turned on him, cutting him with her blue gaze. "That's right. Make fun. That's all you can do," she'd say, and busy herself with the laundry, the dishes, the feeding of animals and children, making a clatter and a show of it, keeping him at a distance lest he see her pain and try to comfort her. "Make fun and babies."

Now he was gone, the children, those stiff-faced, guarded strangers, married, the land sold or leased so she had an income. Not much, but enough. She'd learned frugality at her own mother's knee. She had the house, the garden, a black dog, a yellow cat, and time. All the time in the world.

A door slammed. She heard the shrieks of the twins as they burst through the gate. None of hers had ever made such awful sounds. What was the matter with kids nowadays? And Fern always acting like they were perfect.

The yellow cat slipped under her bed, and she spoke to it, laughing. "Lucky you," she said.

Then the twins came in trilling, "Gramma, gramma," holding out sticky hands in expectation of hugs, kisses, a seat on her wide lap.

She knelt slowly, not being as agile as she had been, and held out her own arms. The children were, after all, kin, and one suffered relatives because of ties of blood. Why you put up with people who were nearly strangers to you in spite of being related, she didn't know, had never thought about. Now she shook her head and put the question carefully away to think on when she had time.

"Turkey day," she said cheerfully, her face so close to

theirs that she could smell the chocolate they'd eaten on their breath. "Can you say, 'Happy Thanksgiving'?"

Boy and girl looked at each other for courage and permission. "Happy Sanksgiving," they said in unison and shrieked with laughter.

Over their bobbing heads she saw Fern and Tom standing awkwardly in the living room as if the old chairs and worn rugs, the cluttered table tops and baskets of books, pine cones, stones and plumes of grasses were somehow threatening to their ideas of taste and order.

Fern, she observed, looked like her own mother—tall, gaunt, plain as a pie plate. Come to think of it, Fern had always acted like her, reserved to the point of heartlessness.

Emma smiled wryly at the comparison, remembering how often her own passionate nature had exploded in the face of her mother's lack of response. It was as if she never had a mother, she thought, her eyes widening. As if she, herself, had never been Fern's.

"Ma?" Fern looked at her, questioning her stillness.

Emma got slowly to her feet. "Oh, I'm alright," she said. She brushed off the knees of her blue pantsuit and looked ruefully at the dust. "The wind's been up all week. No sense sweeping. It just comes back on you. I was just thinking how much you look like your Grandma Evans. You gave me a turn, standing there."

Tom came and gave her a kiss. "As long as she doesn't act like Grandma Evans," he said.

"Heaven forbid." She gave him a hug in return, enjoying the smell of tobacco that lingered on his skin, in his clothes. It put her in mind of how cigarettes used to taste out in the open after a long day chasing cows. Always there would come that moment when, tired, dust-covered, sweat-streaked, you could pull up and relax a bit, look out over the valley that rippled like a live thing, and the wind cooled you and fanned the tiny ash, and everything came together—land, sky and the human heart—just for a second, just long enough to put a stamp on memory.

She let him go and stepped back, shaking her head. "Oh dear," she said. "I'm ready except for my purse. Let me go find it. I won't be but a minute."

Explanations wouldn't do. She turned and went into the bedroom where she dabbed her eyes and threw back her shoulders. She'd been through this all before, a thousand times. Her feelings embarrassed people. They laughed or stared at the ground until she got hold of herself, became Emma again, the Emma they knew, which wasn't who she was at all.

She drew a quick breath. Wasn't it odd? She'd never thought of herself as split in half, but she was, two-sided like the twins, one face turned in on herself, and one turned out for the others. And it was the solitary self she felt best with, had leaned on all her life without anyone knowing, even herself.

She picked up her tote bag with a sigh. Perhaps they could eat quickly and she could get back home in time to feed the skunks and watch the moon come up. So many new ideas. They nearly took her breath away, coming so fast.

"Can we get back by around five?" she asked them. "The skunks come in then. I've got eight right now born right here on the porch."

"Ma, for heaven's sake!" Fern's skin was tight over her cheekbones with annoyance. "It's Thanksgiving. Forget your chores for once in your life and just have a good time."

"That's no chore," she retorted. "It's fun. They're old friends. Besides, they don't know it's a holiday."

Fern didn't answer, but Tom patted her shoulder. "We'll try," he said. "The kids would like to see them, too."

"They'll have to sit still," she said, doubtful, and pulled the door shut behind her.

"Where's your key?" Fern asked.

"Now you know I never had a key. In fifty years this door's never been locked."

Fern reacted as Emma knew she would. Shocked. Reproachful. Gearing up for a lecture. ". . . addicts, drug runners, hippies, cowboys . . . who knows who you'll find smack in your own living room someday, and us not knowing till it's too late. Honestly, Ma, this has got to stop. I mean it."

"So do I," Emma said, settling herself on the front seat. "Remind me to give you some pear preserves to take back. I've got more than I can use."

"Don't try talking around me. It won't work," Fern said. "We want you to sell out and move in with us, don't we, Tom?"

Tom was steering carefully, eyes on the narrow track. "It might be a good idea," was all he said.

When she was little they'd had taffy pulls in the school yard, the boys on one end, the girls on the other, and they tugged until the pale mass stretched out fine as a hank of hair. She felt like the taffy, pulled in two directions, same as always. There was duty, and then there was the other thing that belonged only to her, and it got pushed further and further away until it was only a kernel, a tiny seed, like those of the parsley she planted beside the back door.

There was a photograph in the box she kept under her bed, one she rarely looked at. It had taken the day they'd gone to the carnival, all of them; herself, the oldest, and the little ones strung out like steps, and her mother in a white dress with her dark hair pinned in a bun. She was standing beside them, straight as a chair back, the way she'd been taught by her mother.

The scene Emma replayed in her head for years afterwards had happened just after the photograph was taken. Her mother counted out nickels from her old black purse and said, "Go get ice cream for all of you. Then wait at the drugstore. I'll be along in a bit."

Except she'd never come, not all that afternoon, not ever again. The woman they knew simply vanished, some said with the carnival, some said on the train to California. She who, correct and unbending, had been a secret to her daughter, remained one—mysterious, elusive, a ghostly

figure she'd called mother, but who, perhaps, was someone entirely different and not her mother at all.

Emma had been ready for Normal School that year, but
instead she stayed home taking the place of the runaway,
cooking, cleaning, caring for the young ones, and always
wondering what she could have done to stop her mother's
flight. She married when she was asked, bore her own family as if in a dream, spent the next thirty years in hard
labor.

"Where's the love?" she asked suddenly.

Fern's voice rose until it sounded remarkably like one of
the twins. "Love? Who's talking about love?"

"I am," Emma said. "And I don't want to talk about it
any more. Let's just go eat."

The restaurant was crowded, the service poor, the turkey, as she predicted, overcooked. The twins played with
their plates and dribbled bread crumbs on the floor while
the adults made idle conversation, Emma wondering why
they had bothered to come out at all. It was almost dark by
the time they reached her gate.

"You'd best get started back," she said. "Let me just run
in and get those preserves."

Fern, who always had to have the last word said, "You
think about what we talked about, Ma. It'd be good for
everybody."

"Oh, I will." Emma patted Fern's arm, and as she did,
she realized that she rarely, if ever, had kissed her children,
in part because it had never occurred to her, and partly
because there was a gap between herself and them, a sep-
aration that was more than physical. She stood there a
minute surprised, and then Tom took her arm.

"I'll check the house. Just to make sure."

"It's really alright," she said. "Nobody comes this far
out. You can't even see the place from the road."

"You know Fern. She worries. So do I."

"No need, but thank you." She flicked on the kitchen
light, crossed the room and stood looking into her cup-

board with satisfaction. The fruits of her garden gleamed back at her, row after row of jars of beans, corn, okra pickles, tomatoes, peach and pear preserves. Come what may, she had enough to eat.

"Sometimes I wish we all could live out here," Tom said over her shoulder. "It always looks so comfortable." There was a longing in his voice that she'd heard before and that made her wonder about his relationship with Fern.

She shook her head. "You're city folks. Fern always was. She never fit, just like I'd not fit in town."

"I know. But still . . ."

"You've got your lives. I've got mine. Don't change me. Don't try."

She handed him a shopping bag which he held carefully by the bottom. "Take care, Em," he said, and went out the door and across the squeaking boards of the porch, carrying his parcel as if it were jewels.

The noise of the motor receded up the lane, but their voices lingered, chasing around in her head. Lord, but these visits were tiring!

She sat down heavily on the bench beside the door and fanned herself with her hand. "Where's the love?" she had asked.

Now she answered her own question. "Nowhere."

The simple fact was that she didn't love them any more than they loved her, but none of them wanted to admit it. Duty drove them, made them irritable, gave them something to complain about, something to do when they felt guilty over the lack.

Whose fault was it? Hers? Theirs? Had no one she knew ever loved anyone or any thing to the depths of being?

Maybe love was something dreamed up by people who wrote books, a fairy tale designed to give hope to the hopeless, like the notion of heaven. One thing was sure, you couldn't force it or demand its appearance.

"Emma, for Lord's sake, don't take on so. You expect too much." Her mother's voice came back to her, reflecting, in its faint tone of distaste, her inability to understand or even accept a nature different from her own.

That was the Christmas she had begged for a book of poems, prayed for it until, the words dancing in her head, she believed it would be there for her on the day. What she found, instead, were a pair of boots, wool stockings, and an orange. What she unwrapped, in the plain room, un-decorated, uncared for, was a sense of loss so great a part of her seemed cut off and left to die. As, indeed, it had, while her family scolded, laughed, and at last ignored her for lack of anything better to do. What remained to her was a caring for the shapes and creatures of earth, things that needed no obvious care—the impudent blooming of cactus, the grassy valley, the red rocks and the sky.

Blood ties didn't count for much, she thought, lifting her face to follow the rising moon. It was ties of the heart that mattered, whether they bound you to people or to some other, as she was bound to the land. It was hers. She tended it, cared for it, and was repaid in all the ways that counted.

She thought of the food on her shelves, her moments of seeing, and as she did the windmill caught the moon and spun like a giant silver dahlia against the dark sky.

The motion dazzled her, and the purity of the light. She stretched out her arms, framing the whirling blades be-tween her hands, feeling the dance of blood in her veins, the quickness of her breath, the rising momentum of her body pierced through by what she, yearning, gave the name of love.

Mirage

A wire fence and a row of cottonwoods separate the ranch from Mexico where, in the blue distance, a desert of rock, many-colored, many-shaped, folds in upon itself.

The ranch house is old. Its tin roof slants sharply over adobe walls; a porch runs round it. Inside it is always cool, washed by the wind from the South and shaded by cottonwoods that quiver in the moving air, patter like clapping hands.

The boy beneath them looks up with an odd expression as if he is seeing something hardly visible to the eye. He hums to himself, a tuneless murmuring like wind in wire fences.

From the kitchen his mother watches and wonders if they have done right, bringing him here. He seems so insubstantial, so much a part of the shade, as if he will vanish into it and disappear. Then there would be only two of them—herself and her husband—locked in the bowl of the valley. She does not think she could bear that—the silences between them, the emptiness, the rooms chased by the wind.

Ed was born to this life of cattle, heat, sparse conversation. She has never known for what she was born or where she belongs. She has allowed herself to be moved here, there, everywhere in deference to the wishes of others.

When she and Ed were first married and living in town, she carved out what she felt was a place. She decorated the small house with curtains, ruffles, ineffectual ornaments. "Dust catchers," Ed called them, but they pleased her because she possessed them. She had been happy then, happier still when she became pregnant, tied to another life. But the child, this boy staring up at the trees, was not normal. His mind refused to be captured. He smiled with terrible vacancy, for no reason, and as he grew he began to wander, fearless of the menaces of the city.

To protect him, and to satisfy Ed's longing for the life he remembered and loved, they came here, where the only dangers were space and loneliness, the shimmering fingers of heat, the endlessness of desert. Here the boy still wanders, although they have laid out his boundaries, fenced him in. She keeps watch during the course of her chores, stopping to locate him in the yard, listening for the tuneless sound of his voice as he sings.

"Oh," she thinks, "it isn't fair!"

And she answers herself as she often does. "Did you expect it to be?"

Yes. She had. And that is the trouble. She had expected to move from one dream to another, to be placed in comfortable houses, rooms, streets with names. But this is no dream, not even a nightmare. It is living, relentless, never-ending, and sometimes she thinks she cannot bear it.

"Ford!" she calls, her voice sharper than she intended, a razor blade cutting through the waves of heat. "Ford, come get some juice."

At the sound of his name, the boy turns slowly. He stares, smiles, remains motionless, held by the space between them.

"You come right now," she says. Her fists are clenched on the sill as if she will batter the unseen dimension. "We'll go swimming after awhile?" It is a question, a lure. She holds her breath and feels it blocking her throat.

The boy comes toward the house. He loves to swim, to splash the water in great sheets, frightening the ducks whose takeoff shatters the blue surface, the almost visible air.

"Swim," he says from the doorway. "Swim." He towers above her.

How, she wonders, did she, with her small body, her quick movements, give birth to him? From where has he come, from what ancestor, what twisted gene, what accident? If she knew, she could lay the blame elsewhere, could take pride in her femaleness, in her breasts, her bones.

There is love in her. It feeds upon itself and upon the boy. What will happen when it is gone and none is left? She touches his cheek. It is hot and wet. "Cool off a little first," she says.

In his fist he holds a small wooden cup with a ball tied to it by a string. He is fascinated by his attempts to toss the ball into the painted bowl. He tries now, frowning, forgetting the juice, the promise of a swim.

"Ford. Come on. Drink your juice."

Sensing her agitation he does so, amiably, then looks at her. "Swim?" he says.

"In a bit. You're all hot and sweated. Go sit in the shade till I get dinner in the oven." She isn't sure how much of what she says makes sense to him except by his obedience.

He goes out, banging the screen door.

"Wait for me now," she calls.

His shoulders move in assent.

The shade makes patterns, ripples, sounds. Leaves pull on their stems, patter like rain. Except there is no rain. The sky is hot, blue, cloudless, cupping all in its fist like the bowl cups the ball when he makes the right motion. He tries and misses, tries again. In frustration he looks across the fence to the desert.

The rocks hunch like cattle and give off heat. They change colors as he watches like a kaleidoscope slowly turning, now ochre, now rose, now blue and lavender. Oh, they are such pretty things!

The distance calls like a lake of blue water, larger than the pond and filled with mystery. He walks toward it humming, then climbs the fence and disappears down the deep and stony wash.

The ground is rocky and unfamiliar. He trips once, rights himself, trips again and falls flat. He lies still for several minutes, distracted by the flowing of ants on the ground by his face. They shine like amber, string out like a necklace of beads.

A feeling of space comes to him as he watches, of the rise and fall of earth, of a multitude of shapes, colors, and motions, and he struggles to his feet, arms outstretched, yearning for difference, for change, for fluidity of body and tongue denied him, recognized only as tears in the hollow place where pictures dance and vanish.

In vain he searches for his toy, but it is hiding somewhere in the sand as things so often do, and he cannot find it. He kicks at the ants, scattering them, then he walks on, humming, reaching to shake the bells of the occasional yucca blooming above his head, the ocotillo flowers that lick with teeth of flame.

His mother straightens from the stove and pushes her hair behind her ears in an unconscious gesture. She goes to the window and sees the yard, the fence, the shadows of trees, and at first she is surprised by the emptiness, by the terrible facelessness of the scene as if it has lost its character and has no reason at all for being there.

She stands quite still, clutching the edge of the sink, not thinking, aware only of fear filling her body. She smooths her hair again, feels it, wiry and damp, feels the bones of her skull, her cheeks, the fragile curl of her ears. And she looks down at herself, small and neat, at her narrow feet in their old shoes, and the fact of her body surprises her, too, gives her the impetus to move across the room to the door.

"Sit in the shade," she said. He might be anywhere—in the barn or rocking on the porch, staring South as he does so often, his eyes vacant.

"Ford!" she calls and listens intently. The porch is empty, the chair rocks itself, the wind bells chime sweetly with the sound of a thousand, uninhabited miles.

The barn is deserted, too, but she stands inside calling, her voice higher each time until it cracks with failure. She runs out, looks in all directions, over the rise and fall of the grass, the blue of the water, the heat like liquid glass in the air.

And then, because he is hers, because in this place of few words they have become in some way similar, sharing an instinct like animals in a herd, she knows where he has gone.

She climbs the fence and descends the steep slope into the wash, tracking him, tasting the air, her lips drawn back from her teeth, her eyes narrowed against the glare. She finds the spot where he fell, his toy a few yards further on, and she takes courage from the familiarity of it, moving on nimbly, surprising herself with her agility, the sharpness of her senses.

"Isn't it odd?" she asks herself, aware of her surefooted-ness even as she absorbs the waxen beauty of yucca flowers through a sense not sight.

And then, "What if he's dead? What if he died out here?"

She shakes her head. No. She will not permit his death for without him she has nothing. She needs. She gives him life, and in exchange he gives her a reason, a dignity. Imperfect as he is, he is hers, as is the guilt.

"No one like that in my family," Ed has said more than once. "Not a one."

And now, when he comes to her, they are remote, stiff, afraid of another child, a deeper hurt. Always he takes her in silence, and when he has finished she turns on her side, wrapping her arms around herself and pretending sleep.

The time when they lay secure in each other's arms belongs to the memory of someone not herself, someone she cannot remember, a woman who laughed and sang and came willingly to love.

When Ed speaks these days it is not out of love or even companionship, but with a baffled rage.

"Let's send him away," he says. "There are places. Let's be the way we were."

Across the burned-out plain that divides them she hears and shakes her head. "We can't be the way we were. We're somebody else. And we'd never forget. We'd hear him calling."

Once, last week, he'd put his hands on her shoulders— big hands, rope-scarred, brown as leather—and shaken her so her head swayed like a dark flower. "Goddammit, Em. I could break you in half!"

She'd stared at him, scornful of violence. "Go ahead. See what that gets you."

Hateful words. Hateful acts. Neither of them winning, only drifting further apart.

The sun has moved West. Shadows are long in the folds of the mountains. Infinity, that multitude of openings and closings, of shapes and roads and sounds heard and lost, overwhelms her.

"Nothing is ever the same," she thinks. "Nothing repeats."

She walks on, stopping once beneath ocotillo flowers burning against sky. A bee wriggles out and takes flight, leaving the nearly translucent tongues diminished, vulnerable, and seeing them she sees her own frail rage, her dependency on an environment as unstable as quicksand, as capricious as drought.

If she turns back now, if she goes home, what will happen?

"He's gone," she could say. "I couldn't find him."

Perhaps he will never be found. Others have disappeared here, lost forever, sand sifting over their bones. The boy, too, can become memory, a blurred voice, a shape slipping across the dark mirror of the past.

She puts up her hand. The flowers blaze in her palm, and their beauty strikes her, the violence of life; her own, Ed's, Ford's. Squaring her shoulders she turns South again, pushing against the heat.

The boy's feet seem rooted in earth. His dust-covered sneakers look up at him, untied, smiling cruelly, refusing to move. His feet are heavy. His body is heavy. And the water is far away, though he can hear it lapping the shore, cool and compelling, "Shush! Shush!" like the sound of his heart.

Denied even the simple pleasure of motion, he puts his head back on hunched shoulders and howls, and the sound is that of an animal despairing. Again he cries, and again, unable to stop himself, unaware of the possibility. The echoes bounce back, ringing him with his own pain.

Her ears are fine-tuned. She hears his plea and alters her course, running lightly over the rocks. "It's alright!" she calls. "I'm coming."

She finds him squatting on the ground, arms around his knees, so trapped he does not recognize her but hides his face in fear.

"Ford," she says, stroking his hair. "It's me. Let's go home."

He does not move, or cannot, although he lifts his head and his lips struggle to give shape to sound. "Ma. Ma . . . ma."

"Come on. Get up." She tugs at him. It is like uprooting a tree, but she manages to put his arm around her shoulders and move him a few steps.

Impulsively, foolishly, she came out without a canteen, without her hat or her pistol which hangs beneath her jacket on a hook by the back door. In this place of rock and sand death can strike without warning, dripping yellow venom, flaying with the whip of heat. And these days there are the driven men, the smugglers carrying and receiving drugs, who have no care for any lives but their own.

"Oh, God," she says, her feet sinking into the sand. She

is not aware that she has spoken or that she has prayed. Her throat is dry, scourged by thirst and her constant words of encouragement.

"A little more now, and we'll get a drink. You can have a shower and go to bed."

He whimpers and stops, leaning on her.

"Yes. A drink. The pond. You love the pond. Come on. Take a step. For me."

Instead he looks mutely behind him and begins to cry, catching his tears on his tongue.

"We will both die," she thinks bitterly. Two bodies side by side, stripped of flesh and buried, and for what? Because of her guilt that has blinded her to the needs of others.

"I'm not ready to die." The words form in the haze behind her eyes and travel down through synapses and nerves filling her with fury. She has been cheated—and she has cheated—giving to herself in the guise of caring for this boy who is burying her with his sweat, his weight, his tears.

There are words she has never spoken, half-formed gestures never completed. There is a life beyond dreaming and nightmare and for her it is untouched, a glimmer that lures as surely as the dance of distant heat. How can she allow death when she has never, truly, been alive?

Her voice cracks like the pistol she left behind. "Damn it, Ford! MOVE!"

He turns and stares at her, amazed.

"Move!" she yells again. "Move or I'll leave you here. You understand me?"

Her urgency flicks at him, propels him forward shuddering under his own bulk until she takes his hand and they go on together, slowly as ants or turtles, reduced to minutiae by the darkening sky.

After a journey she can never, later, recall, they reach the wash and stumble down the sides, careless of avalanche or hunting snakes, then look up at the wire fence, almost invisible in the dusk.

Suddenly the boy crumples at her feet. She scrambles on alone, her breath short and hard.

The house, the trees, the barn are unchanged as if she had never left. In the last light, Ed is searching pointlessly, and he seems smaller than she, unable to control the panic in his voice as he calls her name, drawing out the syllables so they hover in the air.

"E-em. E-em . . . where are you?"

She does not answer immediately, but stands on the crest absorbing the scene; the lone figure trapped like a moth in the spill of the yard light, the man, diminished, seeking the familiar, the rudder on which he depends.

"Nothing ever repeats."

She puts out her hands to steady the image, print it deep within herself, a sweetness to be resurrected in times of need.

"Em . . . where are you?"

Her heart begins to race. It hammers against her ribs that seem as dry, as weightless as a bird's at the end of a long migration.

Around the pulse in her throat she calls to him. "Here! Over here. Come help me home."

Marvel Bird

You stand looking at the shack where you lived, where dreams were supposed to happen and didn't, and you're split in half, like in a mirror, watching yourself, Marvel Bird, saying goodbye.

You go through the rooms, thin, dark shadow, kneel to straighten the covers on the mattress that served you and Larry as a bed. You grimace as you look at it—the grimy quilt, the old pillowcases even the sun can't bleach.

"Get up! Get up!" you want to scream at yourself, but disgust is thick in your throat. You turn your back, look out to the mountains, to the valley mottled red, yellow, dun, the hills rounded like the hips of a woman.

You were born in this valley. It is in you, and it calms the way a mother should calm, or a lover. A sweetness runs through it, pacifying you. Ever the fatalist, you shrug your shoulders. "Ah," you say. "Ah," and the sound comes out like wind in cottonwood leaves.

You water your plants a last time, standing in the middle of the porch you built with your own hands out of old two-by-fours and sheets of plastic. The plastic is ripped now, rotted by sun. You were proud of your room at first, though

Larry laughed at your efforts. "What's wrong with the rooms we've got?" he kept asking. But this was your place with green things in it reaching toward light.

Life with Larry Mallory had once held such promise. A room of your own and space to grow. A pasture for the horse you were raising from colthood. No more miner's shack, a room shared with three sisters and the old Indian woman, your grandmother, who passed down to you her thick black hair, her magic with growing things . . .

You were sixteen, and your hair hung to your waist in a braid thick as a man's arm. You were in the patch of garden behind your father's house weeding, watering, forcing life out of the cracked earth by will. And you were listening to your dad and Larry who sat on the porch talking about the smelter closing, and your dad with eight mouths to feed.

That was the evening that Larry stopped on his way out of the yard and looked at you a long time. His eyes were blue as grandma's turquoise naja. That was what you saw. Maybe that was enough.

"The rains don't come, that little bit of water won't help," he said finally.

And you said, "Can't anybody around here talk about anything but the weather? Can't anybody say something good?" Then you bit your lip, feeling tears behind your eyes and something rising inside like bread sealed in an oven.

He pulled back at that, and his blue eyes got round. "Hey," he said. "Hey, now. I was just passin' the time."

"Go pass it someplace else, then," you said, and you felt mean.

Your grandmother said, "Your tongue could cut rope."

Your mother was silent. She was always silent, as if she had no tongue at all, or no words for what she felt.

"You got no cause to speak to my friends that way." That was your dad, embarrassed because a daughter of his had a tongue like a knife.

"Him and his blue eyes and dumb talk," you said. You tossed your braid and left the house, taking the old trail out into the valley where larks rose up singing from under your feet, and the ocotillo scratched the sky with flame. They grew on each side of the trail like trees lining a street, but they cast no shade except thin shadows that crisscrossed in the dust.

"Smart mouth," you said to yourself, remembering his blue eyes under raised brows, and you let the tears come, all the way to your lips.

The next time he came, you apologized.

He said, "Hey! It was nothing. No need getting upset."

You looked at the ground and saw that his boots were worn, a chunk of leather missing from one toe.

"I got a new car," he said. "I'll take you for a ride."

You went with him up the mountain to watch the sunset. The sky and earth changed colors so fast you couldn't keep up and reached out with your hands to catch the swirling.

"You like dancing?" he asked, watching you.

"I don't know." The idea frightened you. "I never tried."

"Come on then." He sat you in the jeep and drove fast, a cloud of dust behind; drove to Obregon's Cafe where he brought you a beer and then another, and whirled you around the wooden dance floor till you were dizzy, light as a leaf, a dust devil touching down.

That's when you started to laugh and couldn't stop. It spilled out and over him till he laughed too, crinkling his eyes. "You're something," he said. "You really are. Old Man Bird's daughter." He shook his head in wonder.

In the car you let him touch you, forgetting all the words of caution you'd heard, the whispers of women, the bulging shame of those who'd fallen. You looked down at your breasts in surprise as if they'd just grown there, pale in the moonlight, your hair spilling across them, a dark stream.

"Marvelous Bird," he said. "Marvelous Bird." And you laughed again deep in your throat, reached out for him as you'd reached for the falling sun.

He courted you then, promised you a house, a bed of

your own with only him in it, a horse to raise and ride, free as the wind. You believed him and held on to that belief for years.

"Men are often fools," your grandmother told you. "Making promises they don't keep and babies to hold you." She told you how to stop a child from being conceived, and you listened.

Your mother said nothing, though she sewed on your wedding dress, pinned it around you, humming a song that had no melody, like the song of the wind in the fences.

For a wedding present, Larry bought you a horse, a wild-eyed spotted thing you loved like a child, like part of yourself, the part tied to earth and leaping away.

"Name him well," your grandmother said. She breathed her breath into his nostrils and spoke quietly to him, soothing his excitement.

You called him Naja after the turquoise crescent on her necklace, and after Larry's eyes.

The trailer where you went to live after the wedding had three rooms, a yard filled with prickly pear, and a pasture with tall grasses for the colt to eat. You loved him; you thought you loved Larry, even when the smelter closed and he had no work. Even when he refused to look for another job and sat every day in the kitchen reading old newspapers, the television casting blue shadows across his face.

That was when you built this room for yourself, setting in two-by-fours, lining it with plastic. You filled it with plants you dug in the fields or begged from the neighbors, and you nurtured them as you nurtured Naja who followed you like a dog, let you lead him, lift his feet, brush his dark mane and tail.

You planted a garden, putting in long rows of seeds in the light of the growing moon, and you bought five black hens and a cock with bronze feathers. You had your mouth to feed, and Larry's, and you did the best you could, feeling fury as you dug, wanting to crack the pale eggs in your palm. You thought about promises and lies, and your mouth curled down and stayed that way.

And you got a job exercising horses at Cy Epperson's training stable. You were unafraid on horseback, and you could steal grain for Naja who ate the strength from your hand.

"That's no job for a woman," Larry said, lifting his head. "For my wife."

"What is?" you asked, staring at him, wanting to shake him in his chair. "You took my place here, so I've got yours."

Months passed. Years, reckoned by the blooming of plants; the ocotillo by the gate, the yucca bending down, the gaudy faces of sunflowers in the ditches, and you wondered why you were here at all, tied to a stranger who seemed to waken only at night when you went to bed, a stranger whose fingers repelled you.

One evening you went out and rode Naja into the mouth of the sun. You rode to the track and let him run free, the way you did with the colts you trained. He needed no urging, thrust himself forward like a bird and flew, so fast you couldn't count the markers, could only hold on, blinded by his mane in your face.

"Whose horse is that?" Cy Epperson said when you drew up.

"Mine," you said, knowing you had wanted him to discover you, had planned it in some dark corner of your body. "Mine. I raised him."

"Best leave him here. We'll train him with the rest."

"I can't pay." You couldn't see his face in the twilight, only the shape of his head against the sky.

"Pay me when he wins," Cy said, and you heard laughter in his voice. "Let's cool him off. Then I'll drive you home." He was young, good to look at, with white teeth and flashing eyes.

"I'd better walk," you said. Hope was in you, and it

needed the coolness of night, the farewell songs of larks for strength.

You needed strength, for at home Larry questioned you, forced you, held you down and took you hard and hurting as if to prove you his property.

You tasted blood on your lip, your tongue. "If you touch me again, I'll kill you," you said, wondering what had happened to that girl who had dared to hope, to the man whose eyes had once held the sky.

He reached out a hand as if to hold you off. "Now wait," he said. "A husband's got rights."

That made you laugh. "So does a wife," you said. "Think about that." You pulled your knees up to your chin, guarding yourself, and watched him pace the room, his movements awkward.

When he stopped and turned to you, his face was cold. "Your trouble is, you think you wear the pants around here. You ever think about that?"

"Every day of my rotten life. And jumping me won't change it." You hurt in places you'd forgotten. There would be bruises on your skin come morning; more sliced into your heart.

"Bitch," he said. He sounded like you'd hit him. You wished you had.

"I'll kill you," you said again. Your hands curled into claws told you it was true.

"Bitch." The sound echoed in your head. You had no defense against his weakness.

In the morning he was gone, your money with him, and though you watched the road for a few days, he didn't come home again.

After awhile you walked a little straighter, swinging your braid. You caught yourself singing now and again. Behind the mask of your face, you began to plan, hoarding your money, hiding it in the earth behind the chicken house, dreaming it in your sleep touched by the moon.

You smiled at Cy. Around him your body rippled like a stream, but you stayed remote, giving hunger a chance to grow. And this, too, you did at a distance from yourself. You were two women—Marvel Bird the guardian of the other who was gestating, waiting to be born.

Sometimes you questioned yourself, but not too hard. It was better not to think, better to be moved by the feel of air, the tug of the moon, voices that never lied but kept their promises year after year.

This year the summer rains came in the spring. The pastures turned green, the horses fat. Naja was sleek, muscled, three years old. Beneath you he ran easily, like the wind.

"He'll win," Cy said. "By God he will." Cy was packing for his trip to the races, and you were helping, trying not to look as the trunks filled. You were trying not to look at Cy's back in the blue shirt, or at the way his hair curled on his neck.

When you didn't answer, he looked up, reading your eyes as easily as you read signs of weather. "What are you going to do while I'm gone?" he asked.

You shrugged, tried to smile. "Keep an eye on things. Maybe get a job down at the beauty parlor."

He stood up, his face level with yours. "You, sticking your hands into old ladies' hair. I'll be damned if I'll let you."

You said, "You sound like Larry. 'Don't do this. Don't do that.' I do what I have to." Then you wanted to cut off your tongue.

You walked away, stood by the water tank and looked down into the dark water where your face swam calling for help, where a white moth floated, a lost flower, on the surface. "Alone," they said. "Alone." Then Cy's face merged with yours and the calling stopped, sinking to the bottom like a stone.

"Come with me," he said. "Naja needs you. I need you."

You knew what you needed, or the other Marvel did. Inside you she was kicking out, shoving to be born. You said, "I'm afraid."

"Don't shut out living," he said.

Inside you hands were clapping. Leaves stirred. Inside you were birdsong and a pain where your heart beat in its cage. You felt the bones around it, brittle and bending, while outside the world flowed like a stream toward an end.

In his eyes, dark as tank water, you saw yourself on the edge of dreaming. "Where is living?" you asked him. "Is it inside or out?"

He shook his head. A smile tugged at his mouth as if he were amused and trying to hide it. "Both I guess," he said. "But that's up to you. To the person."

He put his hands on you, and you moved to meet him, feeling that you'd come to a rock, midstream, that you could hold to it awhile and let the water rush around you.

"I'll come then," you said. Or maybe it was the other Marvel Bird who said the words and who remembered the moth. Stooping, she lifted it with her finger and let it rest there, drying its wings.

Acts of Mercy

She pulls back the curtains and stares down the road. She can tell if anyone is coming by the dust that whirls out over the fields. She sees only the fields now, tall, pale grasses leaning in the wind.

She listens to the wind in the screens, to a lark defying the noon sun. "What if something happens? What if he doesn't come home?" She frowns, annoyed at her tremulousness. It is foolish to fear. She is happy here with Ben, with the colors of distance, yet in that happiness she walks the edge of a knife. She looks toward the road again. Nothing moves.

She gets up, rinses her cup in the sink, and goes out and down the path to the corral where the new horse is standing. He neighs for the others, then he comes and nuzzles her breast through the rails.

"Hello, Sugar," she says. She listens to the sound of her voice, a pebble dropped into the wind.

Ben didn't say when he'd be back. He had shopping to do, a sympathy call to make, slipping an extra ten dollars into his pocket to give to the new widow, a woman no longer young, hiding her fears with hennaed hair and stripes of blue eyeshadow.

The horse nuzzles her again, impatient for attention. He is young, huge, newly broken. "Don't fool with him if I'm not around," Ben said.

"What if . . . ?" she begins, then hushes herself. She takes the horse's head and presses it close.

She hears the ring of the telephone, once, twice, five times, and she runs up the path toward the house. As she reaches the door, the ringing stops. She stands, breathing hard, wondering whom to call, to question.

The phone rings again, and she pounces on it, her voice as shrill as the sawing of a locust. "Yes?" she says. "Yes?"

The woman's voice is even higher than hers. "Saire," it says. "Can you come quick? It's them wild dogs. They're after the calf, and Wade ain't home."

For months a pack of wild dogs has been running the valley, killing cattle, feeding on them. They are hungry. And they have a taste for blood.

"Ben has the truck," she answers. "Can't you do any-thing? Call the sheriff?"

The voice changes. "No. No. I'm scared."

Rilla is always scared. She is a small, hollow-faced woman. Her husband is a silent man given to swift rages which he quells by beating her. Sometimes Saire can hear her cries over the fields, lonely as the cry of a hawk. At these times she drives her nails into her palms, outraged by her own helplessness.

Now she answers, "Turn a hose on them. Bang a pan. Do you have a gun?"

"I'm scared of guns."

"Damn it, Rilla! Just . . . just . . . Oh, hold on. I'll get there. Meantime, call the sheriff."

She slams down the phone, tosses her yellow braid over her shoulder, takes Ben's rifle from the closet. Then she runs to the corral where the colt stands, head up, impatient.

"Don't fool with him," Ben had said.

But she must.

"You've got to help, Sugar," she says. "Stand still now." He dances, excited by her hurry. His haunches loom over her.

"Stop!" she says. "Stop it, now." She slams the heavy saddle onto his back, reaches under his belly for the cinch. He lifts a foot, and she ducks. "Damn it, Sugar!" She puts her hands on his neck trying to calm him. "I won't hurt you. Easy, now."

He looks at her, and she sees herself mirrored on the convexity of his eyes, a small figure in blue with hair the color of the grass. She wonders if, to him, she appears in miniature, her motions those of a gnat's and as easily brushed away.

Then he turns, lowers his head for the bridle, mouths the bit as if it tastes of salt or sweet. His nostrils widen, showing the lining, soft pink. He is too tall for her to mount easily. She clambers into the saddle, holding the rifle away from herself. If he bucks, rears, throws her, what then? She could lie here all day, and no one would know.

Damn Rilla! Damn women! Damn the fear in them that defeats before the chance is taken. She settles firmly in the saddle. "Let's go, Sugar," she says. "Run it!"

He dances, surprised at her lightness. She slams her heels against him and he begins to lope, then flattens out in a full gallop. Her fear is dispersed by motion. If she thinks now it is strategic; the shortest way, avoidance of unopened gates, fences that will slow the rush. She lets her body flow unchecked into the animal that runs like a river beneath her.

Rilla's gate is open. They go through and down the lane. The house sits hidden by mesquite, its tin roof fired by the sun. Rilla stands behind the screen door waving her arms, a mosquito caught on the wire.

In the pasture Saire sees the dogs, four of them, black, with pointed ears. The cow is done for. Her face is ripped

away, the bones showing through tattered flesh. Yet she
stands guard, moving her horns from side to side in an effort to protect her calf that has run behind her and stands
bawling.

The dogs ring the cow, wait for her to falter. They are silent, light on their dark paws.

Saire slides down, stands panting a moment, then aims
the rifle at the leader. In the second before she shoots, he
looks at her with deep and yellow eyes. She pulls the trigger,
watches as he spins, spatters, light as a leaf. She shoots
again, then drops the cow as well, before the intensity of
her violence hits her. She drops to her knees, shaking.

"You did it! You shot the buggers!" Rilla dances around
her, red hair awry. "Git up. Git up, Saire. Come on in the
house."

"Let me alone for God's sake," she says. She'll kill Rilla,
too, she thinks, for her blood lust, her empty heart.

Rilla tugs at her elbow. "You can't jist sit here."

She snatches her arm away. From that small distance
she sees the two of them—women in a sea of grass, killer
and grave dancer with no power but their own to move
them.

She gets up and looks at Rilla.

"Wade'll have himself a fit over that cow," Rilla says.

Saire wants to shake the little figure. She wants to scream.
She does neither. She has been violent enough. "Listen,"
she says, brushing strands of hair from her face. "The cow
was done for. If you hurry, you can butcher the rest. And
. . ." she grins, "You can tell Wade I'll drop him, too, if he
lays a hand on you again."

Rilla's face hollows out even more. She stares up at
Saire, open-mouthed. "I can't tell him that."

"You'd be surprised what you can do when you have
to." She touches Rilla's shoulder. It feels like the dried
husk of a grasshopper, skin over no substance at all. "You
call if you need me," she says. "I'll tell him myself."

She catches the horse, mounts easily, points him toward home. At the gate she turns to wave, but Rilla is gone. Where she stood there is only dust dancing in the filtered light of the yellow afternoon.

Greywolf's Hoss

By eleven that Saturday morning the bar was about as crowded as it was going to get. I mean you could go clear to California and not find a place as dead as the Hodil Bar and Grill. The most that ever happens is that a carload of tourists will pull in for lunch, or a beer, or a trip to the john, and once in awhile Hodie and Tibbs will come in and we'll get to dancing. Or John Greywolf will get drunk on a Saturday night and come in and beat up on Becky his wife who's the waitress here.

Some waitress she is. Mostly she sits in the corner reading the newspaper, her lips moving after her finger that stops and goes, stops and goes until I yell at her to give me a hand. Then she'll ease up, she's heavy and slow, and shuffle around sweeping or taking orders, her big boobs swaying under her T-shirt that says, "I lost it at New Mexico Tech." She has two of those T-shirts, one red and one bright blue, and she wears them in rotation, week in and week out.

Becky, just like the rest of us, feels she's missing something, but doesn't know what it is, or even where to start looking.

It's easy to feel that way here. One day's the same as the next. Faces never change except to get older, and the road through town doesn't go anywhere except out into the sagebrush until it reaches the mountains. They never change, either, though I've heard strangers say the mountains never look the same twice. As far as I can see, they're just there, cutting us off, sealing us up like bugs in a kid's bottle so we act sort of slow like bugs do, holding on and staring through the glass without seeing anything.

Anyway, that morning started out like all mornings: dead quiet. The widow Price come in at nine and ordered her beer, and Mr. Duffy and Mr. Motherall, the two widowers, come in right after for ham and eggs. They always sit by the window so they can see who's doing what or how many cars are on the road, and then they speculate on whatever they see for the rest of the day.

The widow Price sits right at the bar beside the post that holds up the ceiling. After three beers she leans on it with her eyes closed and finds her mouth with a kind of radar. One of those long hands of hers will come up out of her lap and feel around, easy, for the glass. Then one by one her fingers will close round it and lift it, slowly past her chin till it hits her bottom lip. Then her top teeth come down over the rim and she swallows long and hard as if she's dry as a wash. Matter of fact, that's what she resembles: an empty river bed, cracked, hard, good for nothing but the rain that never comes.

Now you'd think that being as she's a widow, Mr. Duffy and Mr. Motherall would strike up a friendship, or that she'd say a word to them now and again. But she's not made that way. My guess is she wants to die and have it over with, and there's not much she finds amusing or worth any effort. She and her husband moved here to retire, and then he up and died, and she's just shriveled a little more each year, keeping company with her own self and her bottle as if that is good enough or better than folks.

Well, about eleven a car pulled up and a man and a

woman got out, she kind of lean and rangy, and him round as an egg, and they come in and ordered lunch from Becky who passed the slip to me over the bar. Then Hodie and Tibbs come and ordered beers and started the juke box playing. They were arguing over by the pinball machine when old Mr. Motherall said, "Look here! Ain't that John Greywolf on that hoss?"

And we all swiveled to look, all except the widow who was chunking on her glass and taking a swallow.

"Goddamn Indian," said Becky. "He took my tomato money and got a hoss." She shuffled to the door, opened it, and stood looking up at her husband who was sitting tall on a long-legged brown gelding.

"Goddamn Indian," Becky said again. "That money was for new curtains and those pink slippers."

I knew about those slippers. Becky kept a picture of them in her jeans pocket. They were slip-ons, flat and fuzzy and dyed bright pink like some kind of Easter Egg.

The horse rolled his eyes at her till the whites showed.

"Go ahead," she said. "You roll your eyes. You do it."

The horse nosed those boobs of hers, and she swatted him away as if he were an insect. She looked up at John who was quiet-faced but with a gleam in his eye that said he'd like to nuzzle in there, too.

"Why'd you do it?" she said. "Why? That was my money. I grew those tomatoes. An' those chiles. Next time I don't trust you. Next time it's me goes to the market."

"Shut up," John said. "You don't know a race hoss when you see one."

"I know this ain't a race hoss," she said, giving a flounce and putting her hands on her hips. "Who says he is?"

"I do," said John. "This hoss can outrun any hoss at two miles or over."

"Hooo!" Hodie set down his beer and came toward the door belly first. "Hooo!" He walked around the big critter that had ribs sticking out like rakes and hip bones that reared up back of the blanket John sat on. Finally he grinned. "This hoss couldn't take my appaloosa," he said. "Not in two miles. Not in four."

"Huh," said John.

"Hell, my bay can outrun both of 'em," said Tibbs, hitching his thumbs in his belt and rocking back on his heels.

"You want to bet?" says John.

"Damnfool Indian," Becky screamed. "Don't you go making no bets."

"I got fifty says he can take 'em both," said John. He looked at Becky's breasts. "You go wait on your people. This here's a man's business."

"Shoot," said Becky, whose vocabulary has its limits. "Whose money is it, you're so ready to throw it down?"

"You goin' to get it sure, woman," he says, sitting up straight as an arrow.

About then the widow woke up and looked at me with those blue and watery eyes of hers. Her old hands skittered across the bar like leaves.

"Are they going to race?" she asked in her papery voice. "Are they?"

I shrugged. "Probably. Ain't much else to do today."

"Where?" She was kind of breathless. She hadn't put so many words together since I'd been tending bar.

I shrugged again. "Maybe out on the Plains," I said. "There's plenty room there."

She scrabbled in her purse with her leafy fingers, pulled out her wallet, dropped the change all over. She had to go crawl for it, and I helped. While we were scrambling around under the stools and tables, she said, "I want to go. I want to see the race. I want to bet."

"Why sure," I said. "You go. We'll get Mr. Motherall to take you." I thought that was a good idea, kind of bringing the old folks together in a common cause so to speak.

"Who's running?" she says. "Whose horses?"

Just then, the egg-shaped man pounded on the table. He was cross and I couldn't blame him. "Are we going to get those hamburgers or not?" he said. He was real ugly when he frowned, his eyebrows running together down his nose like two caterpillars.

"Why sure," I said. "I'll get right to it. Soon's I find out about this hoss race."

"Race!" he yelled. "Is this a restaurant or a book joint?"

I thought that was a pretty clever thing to say, so I grinned at him and at his wife who was leaning back in her chair like she was enjoying it all.

"Well," I said, "you could've come in here pret' near any day in the last five years and this would've been a restaurant. Today's different." I waved my hands at him to calm him down. "I'll get your lunch soon's I find out where this race is going to be. You might consider coming along if you ain't pressed for time. Tibb's big bay is some hoss."

"Let's go, Sam," the wife said. "Let's go see a real race. Cowboys, Indians, and all."

I figured that as soon as Hodie and Tibbs realized they were on stage, they'd put on a real Wild West Show for this lady and her husband. Keep them so interested they'd never know the hamburgers were slow in coming.

"Hey Hodie," I yelled. "This here lady's never seen a real Western hoss race. Where's it going to be?"

Hodie turned, beaming. He snatched off his old black hat and sat down beside the round man. "Why, Ma'am," he said, "This here race is going to be the best you ever saw. We'll start on the other side of the Valley Pass and race to Martin's corrals. Three and a half miles. And my hoss, my Scat, will be there ahead come the finish."

I could see the pair of them getting excited over the idea. Something to tell about back home. I was headed for the grill when I heard the widow. She has the kind of voice that, while it's not loud, sort of undercuts the rest, coming out thin and clattery like a twig covered with ice. "I wouldn't ever bet on an appaloosa," she said, and stood there waiting.

"Why, Ma'am!" said Hodie.

"Why not?" asked the round man, looking the widow up

and down as if trying to assess what she knew and how sober she was.

"Appaloosa's not a breed," she said, kind of jerky like she wasn't used to hearing her own voice. "It's just a mixed-up, spotted horse. Never knew one didn't have something wrong. Some fault. Some crazy trick."

"My Gawd," said Hodie.

"Who'd you bet on, then?" the round man asked.

"That Indian horse. Long-legged. Deep chest. Skinny, but good muscles. Thoroughbred. Used to distance."

"Jeesuz," said Hodie.

"Prayers won't help," said the widow. "Give me a bourbon."

I tell you, I near fell over my feet I was so surprised by it all. I poured her a shot, and she drank it, quick, all in one motion like a man. "Miz Price," I said, "where'd you learn about hosses?"

"Born and raised on a horse farm," she said. "Lost it and came out here. Haven't seen a good horse since." She tucked her purse under her arm. "I'll take the bottle. Might need it."

I handed it across the bar, and she frowned at me. "In a bag," she said. "In a bag. People will get the wrong idea."

I was about to say that there weren't any people out on those Plains and wouldn't be any except us, but I thought better of it. I wrapped the bottle.

"Gentlemen," she said, turning toward Mr. Duffy and Mr. Motherall. It would have been a real elegant move except she was drunk. She slammed into a stool and stood there blinking. "Oh dear," she said.

I hated to see it. I surely did. She'd been so perky there for a minute. So sure of herself. I scooted under the bar. "You ever rode in a jeep?" I said to distract her.

"What?" she said. "What?"

I said, "If you're going out with these two, you're going in that jeep, so you hold on to your purse and that bottle, hear?"

Her face was scrunched up like she was going to cry. "It's no fun anymore," she said. "None of it."

"Sure it is," I said, though I didn't believe it. I could see myself in fifty years all shriveled up and fearful of dying. I could see it plain as anything. I stood there wishing I'd never seen the widow, or this town that's two houses and a filling station, and a restaurant, all swallowed up by grass-lands and mountains and the Plains, and that god-awful blue sky day after day.

Nothing's fair in this world, I remember thinking. Nothing at all.

Mr. Motherall and Mr. Duffy got her settled in the front seat, belted her in so she wouldn't go out the side, and they gave her the bottle and the paper bag for the bet money to hold in her lap. The three of them rode off leaving a cloud of dust that blew in and lay over the tables.

I served up two hamburgers, burned, but I disguised that with some onions and green chiles on top, and I plunked down a fresh pot of coffee at Sam's elbow.

"Best pay now," I said, "so we can go when you're done."

He pulled out a fat wallet. "Who are you betting on?"

I thought about it. Stood there remembering what I knew about those hosses. Tibb's big bay was part Arab and tough. John's gelding had caught the eye of the widow for all it looked like a hay rake. And Hodie's little Scat, as pretty a horse as I ever saw, wouldn't cross water. I grinned. Maybe the widow was right. That hoss could move quick as a jack rabbit but wouldn't get his feet wet. And I knew another appaloosa that would spook at the white line down the road. Dumped plenty on the concrete, that hoss did.

"It'll be between the bay and the Indian if they come to water. More'n that, I can't say."

I took the twenty, counted out change from the register. "I got to get my truck and get my sister to fill in for me," I said. "You can follow me up there or you can go on. Ain't but one road."

"We'll wait for you," the round man said. He counted his

change carefully, debating on the size of the tip. I knew his type. All bluff and bluster till it comes down to it.

"Nothin' to be scared of if you want to go ahead," I said. He looked at me, quick like, and subtracted a sum from what he decided to leave.

I grinned. You get to know folks after awhile.

"You coming?" I said to Becky. She was picking up plates, slopping what was left all over.

"Naw," she said. "You think I want to see my money throwed away?"

"If he wins, you can buy two pairs of them slippers."

"Huh," she said. "Win? That bag of bones?"

"Suit yourself." I went out back to find Lou. She was sitting on the wooden bench by the door reading confession stories and pulling strings of that god-awful grape gum out of her mouth.

"Spit out that gum and come mind the kitchen for me," I said. "I'm going to a hoss race on the Plains."

"You're crazy," she said. "In this heat."

Lou is bone lazy, and slower even than Becky. I'm surrounded by drunks and fools. By this land with nothing on it but cattle and coyotes. I wanted to scream. "Nothing's fun," the widow had said. She didn't know the half of it.

I picked up Sam and his wife whose name was Eleanor, and we headed West through the creek bottom and the foothills.

Somewhere on that road, I turned wild. I mean, the devil was purely into me. There I was in my pickup leading Sam and Eleanor in their shiny Continental on the way to a hoss race. The road stretched out clear as a string. Sam, sure of himself, full of bluster, sat on my tail. I stepped on the gas, watched the speedometer move up to 65, then 70, then 90, and in the mirror I watched old Sam, his round head a bump behind the steering wheel, fall back and disappear.

That truck flew over the dips in the road, took the hills like a good horse, clean and straight, the grass and the flowers in the ditches leaning away like fire. I left Sam standing still, passed Hodie and Tibbs in a two-horse trailer, and, away off to my right, a dark shape that might have been John easing the gelding toward the Plains.

If nothing was fun, I thought, I'd have a time anyway. I'd make my own fun, even if it was only this, racing the road with the wind in my face. Leaving the hawks behind, and the dudes, and the sound of me hollering, urging myself on.

I passed the jeep, too, the old folks setting straight and stiff, choking on a curl of my dust. I went through the Pass and on down without stopping to look. I pulled off where the shoulder was wide. Down below the yellow grass moved. The daisies and the white poppies fluttered. Out at Martin's corrals, a windmill swung round, caught the wind, flashed bright as a silver dollar in the sun. A few cattle hung around the base of the tank, heads down, legs planted square. A few more scattered out along the wash looking for shade.

I sat there for a spell, just looking. There was something about that view; fifty miles of yellow grass, no trees but a few mesquites by the wash, nothing but grass, cattle, and a stream bed. And all around, in the distance, the mountains, blue and purple and changing color under the shadows of the clouds. It was a sight.

I thought maybe it was possible that nothing happens anywhere unless we make it. That the widow was copping out, and Becky, too, and Hodie and Tibb, and even me. Maybe it was only John who had the right idea, spending his wife's money on a dream.

Hodie and Tibbs pulled up behind me. "Hooo," said Hodie. "You can drive some. Where'd you leave the dudes?"

"Coming," I said. "Sam's holding that wheel like the front end's going off without him."

They both laughed, then turned serious. "Let's get these hosses out and walk 'em a bit. Scat hates trailin'." Scat swung his spotted rear and hauled back on his halter.

Pretty soon everybody come up and parked and got out and stood around looking over the course. John rode up, and the widow spent a long time talking to the brown hoss. I could hear her voice, but I couldn't make out the words. The animal listened, pricking up his long ears.

When she come back she said, "Huh!" just like John did.

"Well?" said Sam.

"Well, what?" the widow said.

"Which one?"

She looked at him. "Told you before," she said. She went over to the jeep, reached in, took a drink. "Place your bets and let's get started. I want to see that brown horse run."

They did. Eleanor was so taken by Scat (he is a picture, round-rumped and slick) that she put fifty dollars on him in spite of Sam's frown. He stuck with John, while I put ten on Tibb's bay and so did the two old gentlemen.

The widow shook her head at me and kept on drinking. Only when the three hosses and riders were lined up on the rise did she stop. "I'll drop my handkerchief," she said. "That's the signal." She rummaged in her purse, pulled out a piece of cloth that looked like she'd had it fifty years. She stretched out her arm, her eyes for once bright and focused. The handkerchief spun in the wind, hesitated, dropped.

"Go," she said, in what for her was a shout.

And they did, with Scat moving ahead like a jack rabbit on those black legs. Tibbs held down the middle, and John and the tall gelding were back in the rear sort of holding back like they weren't running at all. John wasn't using a saddle. He was riding Indian style, high up on the hoss's shoulders. I began wishing I'd bet on him instead.

"Smart," the widow said. "Should have had him riding for me in the old days."

The hosses went down the rise and onto the flat, strung out one-two-three, the appaloosa's rump twinkling in the sun, his black tail fanned out behind.

"Isn't he pretty?" Eleanor said.

"Pretty is as pretty does," said the widow.

"Whoop! Whoop!" We could hear Hodie yelling like he was driving cattle. He was happy out there, ahead of them all.

We're all having fun, I thought. This here is fun, no matter what.

"What's that Indian doing?" Sam asked. "I thought you told me his horse could run." His eyebrows were far down on his nose, wriggling.

"Watch," the widow said. She took a drink.

"You could pass the bottle." Sam wiped his hand across his mouth.

"I could," she said, but she put it back into the bag and held on.

"My God," Eleanor wailed. "The bay! Look at the bay!"

Sure enough, Tibbs was making his move on the flat. The bay stretched out his neck. Gobs of dirt, sprays of grass flew out from under his hooves.

Behind them I saw John rise higher on the gelding's shoulders. The length of that hoss's stride grew. With those long legs he covered as much ground with one stride as the others did in two. He ate up distance without thinking about it, like it was easy. Like what he was and was able to do were the same thing so he didn't have to worry or fret or fight the man up there on his neck.

"Shoot," I said. "There goes my money."

"And mine," said Eleanor.

Then the thing happened that made sense out of all the widow had said.

Little Scat still had the lead when they hit the cattle grazing by the wash. The bay was close, but Scat was holding on. The cattle scattered, and the horses went over the edge, and then the bay come up the other side and kept on going. There wasn't any sign of Scat at all. What we could see was Hodie's black hat, just the top of it, rising and falling like he was being tossed in the air. He was.

There was six inches of water down there among the stones. Six inches of water that wasn't even running but was just setting there green and still and harmless. But it was water, and Scat took one look, reared, sunfished, and left Hodie in it cursing for all he was worth.

Scat came up our side, shook himself, twitched his ears, and went to grazing like he knew a joke no one else had heard yet.

"Appaloosas," said the widow. "All crazy."

John and the gelding rose up out of the ditch in one leap, moving faster now, fast as a twister come out of the sky. They ran down the bay and kept going, passed the windmill, Martin's corrals, and went another half mile before they even slowed down.

"Whoopee!" said Sam. Then we all stood there quiet like we'd seen something we knew was going to happen but didn't believe.

The widow emptied the bottle, threw it into the weeds, then retrieved it.

"The only thing I ever knew about was horses," she said. "The only thing."

"You sure know them, though," I said.

She looked at me. Her eyes were glazed again. "It's done now," she said. "Finished. Now we'll all go back there and sit and sit . . ." Her face shook. All the little lines and creases on her skin stood out plain like roads on a map. "What'll I do?" she asked. "What'll I do?"

I stepped back. I'd been happy running alongside that hoss. Now here she was bringing back the emptiness. "I don't know," I said. "I sure can't tell you how to spend your time."

It was mean to say that, but I was feeling mean. I didn't want to hear about her problems when I had enough of my own. I didn't want to think about Becky and her pink slippers, or Lou and her confession stories, or Hodie, come up now all muddy and saying "Hooo," between curses. I plain didn't want to think at all except about how John and that hoss had gone and done something beautiful, and that, maybe, when I got old, I'd remember it: the yellow Plains and the mountains, and the way that crazy Indian's dream brought us all to some kind of life for a day.

"Shoot," I said to her. "I'm sorry."

She shook her head. "I had my time. Wasted it. Didn't believe hard enough. You've got to believe. Take chances. Try, like Greywolf there. Like that old horse."

"Believin's hard," I said.

She screwed off the bottle cap, looked in, shrugged her shoulders, bony as that brown hoss's, and threw the bottle back into the weeds. "It's all we've got," she said.

The Ugliest Woman
in the World

"Aw. C'mon, honey. Please come with me. You *got* to see this, and besides, I'm going to need help. Please, honey."

That's Buck sounding like a little kid the way he does when he wants something. Only I don't want to go with him. I want to sit down, put my feet up, and feel the baby swimming inside me like a goldfish butting the sides of a bowl. It's my baby, anyhow, not Buck's. And I'm my own person. You think he'd understand that, but he doesn't. It's, "Sib, honey, let's do this," and "Sib, honey, let's do that," like he's tied to my apron strings.

Maybe it was a mistake, running off with him like I did, but how did I know? I was pregnant, and Jim was married to somebody else and beating up on me because of it. I thought about going to old Tillie Stops, the Indian woman who lived in a trailer out past town, and getting something to fix it, but I'm funny about taking stuff I don't know what's in it, and besides, I had a friend in high school who died getting rid of a baby.

So I looked around town at the kids I'd gone to school with—cowboys, truckers, drunks—and Buck was the only decent one in the bunch. I didn't have a plan or anything when I waylaid him at the gas pump at the Seven-Eleven that night. I just said what came into my head which was, "You're going to marry me, Buck Flowers."

He gave a hoot and said, "No way, José. I just got rid of Number Two."

"Everybody knows what *she* is," I told him.

He looked at me out of those bright blue eyes, hard blue, like the sky. "What makes you so different?"

"Ha!" I said. "You ever see me bar crawling?"

He switched off the pump. "You got a boyfriend. Why pick on me?"

"Because," I said.

"That's no reason."

"I know what I know," I said.

"What do you know?"

I moved close and looked up at him through my eyelashes. "You and me are crazy," I told him. "Not mean crazy like her and Jim, but wild. We could go places, do things, maybe amount to something."

It sounded good. He screwed the gas cap back on and flipped down the lid, and I could tell he was thinking about what I said because Buck's nothing if not crazy. He likes being that way. It fits his notion of cowboy. Finally he asked, "Where you want to go?"

I shrugged. "Anywhere's better than here."

"You got that right." He laughed, and those white teeth of his shone even whiter in the green light from over the pump. He scuffed his boot back and forth across the dust and stared at the marks he was making.

"You look like an Indian reading sign," I said. "What do you see?"

"Don't call me no Injun," he said, before he remembered I'm half one. But Buck's never embarrassed about anything. He just bulls on through. "I'll tell you what," he said. "I'm leaving here in a couple weeks. When I do, I'll look you up. That way you got time to change your mind."

"I won't," I said. "And if you forget, I'll come after you. Us Indians don't forget promises."

"See you around," he said, and he left me there in the dark, with the wind in my ears and inside me the hope that he meant it.

I hated that town. A feed store, a cafe, a main street lined with bars, and the bare plains blowing away in the wind. I'd been trying to leave it forever, but things kept dragging me back like a bad dream you can't wake up and forget. I'd get a job and then the place would go bust, or they'd lay me off, and there I'd be—back on the bus to Mama.

The one thing I didn't want to do was to move in on her all swelled up with a baby. Not that she'd say anything, she's not that way, but Lord, she didn't need grandchildren. She's still young and pretty, and she's got herself a new husband, and what did they need with a baby?

What I liked about Buck was you never knew what he was going to do next, like when he rode a bucking horse down Main Street and into the Drygulch Saloon, or the time he went out on the Interstate and shot at hippy hitch hikers with his .45 and scared them half to death.

Besides, he's a good hand, easy on his horses, savvy with cattle. I figured we'd get settled on a ranch someplace with room to raise a kid, but getting him settled has been harder than getting a mustang inside a barn. And this country! Cactus and mesquite and a hot wind blowing around the edge of the black mountain most of the time. It comes straight up from Mexico, that wind, and it leaves dust in your mouth and in your hair so you never feel clean. It isn't like what I imagined when Buck and me were beating down the highway on our way to dreamland.

He's been through four jobs in five months, can't keep his mouth shut, doesn't have a lick of sense or respect, and doesn't want any. I can recognize the signs and start packing before it happens.

"Old Jack," he'll say over dinner, "old Jack's dumb as a box of rocks. Can't find cattle spread out in front of him. Can't drive 'em. Can't even stick on a bucking horse."

This last job, they fired him because he set Jack up by

staring at his horse's rear end till he asked Buck what was he looking at. And then Buck says, "Same thing you see when you look in the mirror."

We got our severance pay the end of that week, packed up our dogs and gear and hit the road again. Only the adventure was out of it. I'd just like to have a place I know is mine, and I'm hoping this place is it.

That first time, after he'd come to get me and sat out front revving the engine in his old Dodge pickup and shouting, "Hurry up, Sib!" and me throwing boots and jeans and makeup any-which-way into a sack, that was exciting. We were free and going places, Buck and me and the baby. He didn't know about it then, but it hasn't made any difference. He says he's crazy in love with me, and we're going to have a bunch of kids of our own. He says I'm different from all the rest, and he's always at me for some thing or another. Like now. I'm supposed to go down the road and watch while he puts some old cowboy and his two women off the place.

"You got to come," he says. "You won't believe this. He's living down there with the ugliest woman in the world and her girlfriend."

"I don't need to look at ugly women," I tell him. "Or queers, neither."

"You do! You got to look at this one!" He spins on his heels, and his spurs rattle. "Besides, I'm scared to go back by myself."

"Is the big cowboy fwightened?" I say. "Does him need his mommy wiv him?"

"Now you *quit!*"

He hates it when I talk baby talk to him, even when he's acting like one. For all he's big and handsome and beats his chest like King Kong, I had to teach him how to kiss along with a lot of other things like how to eat proper and keep his elbows off the table.

"Just go tell them and leave me be for once. I'm tired."

"Okay. Be that way. But I won't tell you what she said to me."

"What'd she say to you?"

"I'll never tell." He gets the kitchen table between us and grins like a fool.

I jump at his face with my nails. "You tell me, Buck Flowers!"

"Goddamn!" he says, laughing. "Goddamn! I've got me a wild Injun." He wrestles my arms down and tries to kiss me, but I duck my head.

He makes me so mad so quick with his fool games. "You tell!"

"For a kiss."

"First I want to hear."

He drops my arms and takes his tobacco and cigarette papers out. "Well," he says, slowly, just to aggravate me, "well, she said, Lois, the ugly one, that if I'd come over when old Bill wasn't around she and her girlfriend would show me some tricks I never thought of."

"You never thought of much."

"Hey!" His eyes flash blue. "There's lots of women after me. I don't have to go begging."

"You want to sleep with queers, you go right ahead. Only don't run back and tell me. I'm not interested."

"You asked hard enough." He licks the paper, twists the end, and lights up. "Now. You coming with me or not?"

I sure am. No dyke's going after my man, and that's the truth. "Give me a minute. I'm not going down there looking like this."

He comes after me, his lips all puckered up. "Kiss!" he says. "Kiss! You promised."

"You look like a shoat. Who wants to kiss that?" I say and run for the bathroom.

I get mad while I'm combing my hair, but not at Buck. At this Lois person. "Wolf ugly," Buck called her. If she's that bad, where does she come off making a pass at him, and her with a husband and a girlfriend to boot? I'll show her, or my name's not Sybil Early, and I'm not half Cheyenne Indian on my daddy's side. My real daddy. The child molester. It's true. My mama took me away from him when I was real little, after she found out how he tied me to a chair and made me watch while he burnt my sister's fingers on the stove, but we've heard he's been in jail three times since then. I got my bad temper from him, and my black hair heavy as rope. And right now my temper is boiling. I think that ugly woman needs telling real bad.

We get in the truck, and the dogs, Ringer and Rosie, jump in behind. Ringer rides on the roof of the cab, and I wish he wouldn't, because someday he's going to fall off and get squashed, but Buck thinks it's funny, that dog up there. People stare at us going down the highway, and kids point out car windows, their mouths open. Buck waves back and turns on his police siren, scaring hell out of them.

"You're going to get arrested for that," I tell him.

He just grins. "It's only fun, honey," he says. "Nobody gets arrested for having a little fun."

"That's what you think. And I'm not bailing you out, either."

"Yes you will," he says. "Yes you will because you'll miss me. You'll be laying in that big bed all by yourself, all cold and lonesome and thinking about me locked in a cell with pimps and junkies, and you'll miss me so bad you'll kick the jail house door down."

"Bull," I say and stare out the window at the mountain. It's mostly bare rock, and it rises right up out of the far pasture like a wall. I hate that mountain, I'm not sure why, unless it's because you can't move it, can't cross it, can't do a damn thing with it except go around and leave it there, making a big shadow across the valley floor. Looking at it I always feel like there's something I'm supposed to do, a discovery I have to make but can't get to.

Buck turns off. We bump across a cattle guard. Four scrawny horses come to the barb wire and stand there chewing on wisps of grass.

"Those horses don't look too good," I say.

"That's the truth, but old Bill don't care. That's why he's

fired. Hasn't checked his cattle for a month. I tell you, honey, those women have worked him over so bad he can't climb on a horse."

"You think?"

He nods. "I know. These are baad women."

"You better not let me catch you flirting."

He grins at me. "The day I flirt with them, I'll kiss your ass and give you a week to sell tickets."

He pulls up by a pile of rocks near a trailer that looks like it's on its last time around. The roof is buckled, and there's a crack in the glass door that's been mended with duct tape. A pile of garbage—papers, tin cans, grapefruit rinds— is lying beside the steps like they just toss what they don't use out the door and the hell with it. Over to one side is a rusted pickup and an old horse trailer with the side bars bent, and there's not a tree or a plant or a single growing thing anywhere.

A dog comes around the corner of the house, slinking and growling and looking mean. He ignores Ringer growling from the cab roof, and sniffs my shoes. I back off, not because I'm scared but because he's got extra toes growing out of his two front legs, three of them on each side, and it's disgusting.

"Get me out of here," I say to Buck. "You just take me home right now. This place is sick. This dog is sick."

"It gets better," he says, meaning it gets worse. He knocks on the door, and the glass shakes like it's going to buckle. I can see us standing there while it rains glass.

"Goddamn you, Buck Flowers," I say, and then the door slips back and I don't say anything at all.

She's got hands cracked like buzzard claws, big feet in black high tops, a face like a twisted pine root dug up and left to rot, hair sticking out from under a feed store cap. And she, *it* is going to teach Buck things? Somebody's crazy. It isn't me.

"Bill around?" Buck asks. He's grinning more because of the look on my face than because he's friendly.

"Don' know," she says. Her voice sounds like gravel being dumped out of a truck. "Prob'ly out with them horses. I been busy. Some son of a bitch stole my windmill. I been lookin' for him. Come on in."

I don't want to go in. But if I don't, I'll be standing out here in the rocks with old Three Toes drooling on my boots. I slip in close to Buck and look around.

The other one's on the couch. She's better looking, younger, but she's got these pop eyes like a praying mantis, and they don't blink, just stare—at me mostly. She's eating something; from the smell it's old cheese, and she nods and chews and stares and keeps swinging one leg like she's got St. Vitus Dance and can't keep still. She's got a chain wrapped around her ankle; a big, thick chain, and she sees me looking at it and grins at me till I back away as far as I can, up against the refrigerator.

Buck says, "Hey, Lois, you got any war stories to tell me?"

She cackles. "Got stuff that'd curl your hair, boy. Any time. Any time at all. I told you, din't I?"

I say, "He's got no time." Then the one on the couch glares at me and my jaws clamp shut and won't open. Down deep inside, the baby kicks and kicks like he wants out, and I wonder if there is any truth to those tales about babies being marked by things.

Lois ignores me. "You want a beer?" she asks Buck, stepping close to him.

"No thanks. I got to find Bill. This here's Sybil. My wife."

"Hey," she says like she only just saw me. "You want a beer?"

I shake my head.

"Well I sure do. I been trackin' those thieves, and when I find 'em . . ." she makes a cutting gesture with her scaly hand.

"How'd they take it?" I get out.

She shakes her head. Her hair's so stiff it doesn't move, and this close to me she smells like the cheese. "If I knew, I'd have caught 'em by now, wouldn't I?"

She pushes past me to the refrigerator. Out of the corner

of my eye I see that leg swinging back and forth, the sunlight reflecting off the chain.

Buck say, "I'm going to look for Bill," and puts his hand on the door.

"Me, too," I say. I'm not mad anymore. I just want out, like the baby. The walls are pressing in on me, and the smell of cheese, and the glimpse I just got of the bed in the back room; just one bed, the sheets and blankets crumpled up like used aluminum foil.

The one on the couch says, "You don't have to go, sweetie. Stay and visit awhile," and those pop eyes of hers start rolling like a locoed horse.

I run out that door. If I don't, I'll throw up. I make for the truck like it's home, and I nearly trip over Three Toes on the way. "Git!" I yell. "Git, you son of a bitch!" And I feel my lunch rising in my throat. I sit in the truck with the door open, breathing hard and deep.

"What'd I tell you?" Buck says. "Better'n a freak show, aint it?"

I turn on him. I want to smack that smart-ass face of his. I want my Mama. I want out of it all; this place, my life, always looking and never finding, and hope gone sour in my mouth.

"I hate you so bad," I say to him. "I hate you like a snake." And I have to laugh at the way his eyes go blank like I punched him in the gut.

It's only for a minute, though. Then he starts smiling again like the damn fool he is, can't recognize the truth when it jumps up and bites him. "Aw. Come on, honey. You don't mean that," he says.

I put my head back on the seat and close my eyes so I don't have to see him or anything else; the rusted trailer and that critter watching from the door, the yellow valley, the black rock mountain rising up like judgement.

I think I'm going back to mama, baby and all. Back to someplace where the days begin and end all in one piece, and if nothing exciting happens, well, at least you can sleep at night without dreaming, without a voice coming at you and dragging you awake.

"You all right?" he's asking. "Answer me, honey."

"Go find Bill and leave me alone." I listen to his boots crunching the rocks, and I wrap my arms around my belly like the baby's already come and I can hold it, see its little face like a flower in the sun.

"You and me," I say to it. "You and me will be just fine."

My words spin out the window on the wind, and it's like I go out with them and can see myself sitting here rocking and singing and making promises I might never keep. And I can see me years from now dragging a bunch of kids from place to place like a quail mama followed by her dusty brown babies. I can see it plain as day; me all shriveled up and Buck with his mouth still going, and the kids wearing cast-off clothes and boots too small for their feet. I've seen it all before. Beat down women trying to look young, trying to keep up with their men who don't give a hoot in hell for nobody but themselves.

"Screw it!" I say outloud, and I slide across the seat behind the wheel, turn the key, and shift gears into reverse.

Buck spins around at the sound of the engine, and his idjit mouth flies open. "Where you going? What the hell?"

He starts running, and I start driving fast, raising a cloud of dust he's lost in, even when I hit the blacktop and turn North on the road around the mountain—the road that will take me home.

Learning the Names of Things

There's a *paloverde* tree right outside my door, so close I
have to duck under it coming and going. When I parked
my trailer I planned it that way because it's a pretty tree
and interesting. *Paloverde* means "green stick," and the
whole tree—trunk, branches, twigs—is green, with hardly
any leaves to speak of. When it blooms it looks like yellow
gauze, and the scent hangs on the air like the perfume de-
partment of a store at Christmas.

It's a miracle tree, but these days everything seems mi-
raculous. I look, touch, smell the air, the earth and its
growing things and then carry my sensations inside as if in
a jewel box. No matter what, the contents are mine.

My name is Lily Crewes, but out here on the desert they
just call me Lily. Nobody in our camp has a last name, and
that's fine. It gives us all privacy, freedom, the most important thing of all. I'd guess that everybody here had their
freedom attacked or taken away at some time. We're the
walking wounded with bruised hearts, and instinctively as
animals we've come back to earth to be healed.

None of us talk much about our pasts or our wounds. In
fact, we don't talk much at all. There's a silence here, part

secrecy, part meditation, part a listening to the desert, a natural drug that sends us to sleep without dreams.

I'm a runaway wife. One of those you read about in magazines who disappear without a trace so that no one knows if they're alive or dead. I suppose I might reappear someday just to make everything legal, but then again, I might not. Anonymity is a glorious thing. Without an identity, without the protective coloration of house, husband, visible background, I can say what I want, be what I want with no comments. Take me as I am, or leave me alone. It never happened to me before. Where I came from, everybody wanted to do a make-over of Lily, as if there was some basic lack in me that could be overcome with a lot of prompting and pushing and what amounted to a frontal lobotomy.

When I think about my life, and I often do, trying to make sense out of it by writing in my journal, my past seems like a kaleidoscope, a million pieces of jagged glass tumbling and abrading each other, with me, defenseless, in the middle. Did they draw blood, those knife-edged shards? Sure, but inside where there was no visible scar, just shreds of Lily hanging in there because, no matter what, I knew life could be beautiful and probably was, someplace else.

My mother raised me to be that nebulous creature, "a lady." I say nebulous because, the way she saw it, ladies weren't flesh and blood but fairy godmothers incapable of wrong-doing. If by some chance they erred, there were always the neighbor ladies and the governing body of the world at large to bring them back to perfection.

"What will people think?" was her standard, and while early on I decided that people's opinion had nothing to do with anything, it colored enough of my behavior to get me into trouble in my marriage.

While I led myself to the sacrificial altar, the horror of old-maidhood, the snickers and gossiping of acquaintances, were pushing from behind. "Martyrs to somebody else's cause," is what my neighbor, Meggie, says.

Meggie lives down a little path and around the bend in a

hodge-podge house that she made herself out of old doors, damaged trailer siding, and pieces of tin roof. "Nobody's got a lock on construction," according to her.

We don't see each other often, some mornings for coffee and once a month when I give her a ride to town to cash her social security check. I don't get checks. I've vanished. But Meggie has enough to make do. That's all she wants, she says. That and no one around giving orders.

My money, that I took from our joint account, Robert's and mine, is hidden under the floor boards of the trailer. If I'm careful it will last awhile yet, and I am careful. Me. Lily the consumer! That's what they used to call me; all those women who called themselves friends but who were as brain dead as I was. I used to buy in binges like a food addict; clothes, jewelry, dishes, napkins, towels, bits and pieces for the house, anything that looked good. I had taste, but that didn't count. It didn't cement the pieces of the kaleidoscope or stop Robert's voice from cutting deeper.

Robert is a professor of what is called "Artificial Intelligence." He makes robots play chess and machines talk like people, but he can't talk like a person himself. During the seven years we were married, he became as much a robot as one of his creations, and acted like I was one too—emotionless, programmed, incapable of feeling pain.

I'd be asleep, and I'd hear him coming after me, his voice like a buzz saw. "Lily, Lily, get up. Clean the stove. . . . the tub . . . the cellar . . . wipe the mirrors, dust behind the pictures . . ."

They've got a name for that kind of behavior now—"obsessive compulsive," but then I never gave it a name or even thought about it. I was married. Stuck. Who would believe the "clean behind the pictures" bit? What would people say?

Besides, I was usually too exhausted to think at all. Brain dead. Numb. Abused, though I didn't call it that then.

And then I woke up. Just like that. I caught myself in

mid-stride rushing out my own front door to do an errand and get back in time to finish the list of chores Robert always left for me. It was a day for rejoicing, but I wouldn't have noticed except that a cardinal flew past me, landed on a bush, and sang his scarlet heart out.

How many springs had come and gone and me on my knees mopping? How many sunrises had I missed learning to make perfect eggs and oatmeal, and measuring tea with precision into Robert's blue pot? How many daffodils? Soon I'd be old—I could die tomorrow—and what had I done? Seen? Listened to? I was a stranger to my own heart.

I went back inside, smoked a pack of cigarettes, and thought. I thought for days. Robert didn't notice.

I noticed him, though. I saw things I'd never seen before. He pouted at dinner when the food displeased him, which was often. He was paranoid. He believed the telephone company was after him because I mailed the payment a day late. He was a slob. He left his clothes, both dirty and clean, in piles on the floor for me to sort. He was possessive, selfish, and completely humorless. Even his laughter was fake. "Ha, ha," he'd go and then look to see if the rest of the company was laughing. It was his feet that did it, though. They were ugly and big, and when he walked, the floors shook. I could hear him coming—bang, bang, bang— like King Kong, and it scared me. *He* scared me. Sometimes when he hugged me he left bruises on my arms, and when I cried out he laughed and said, "Oh, you're too fragile." This was love? Not in my book.

So I sold my jewelry, emptied the checking account, took the Cadillac, and left. I drove off into the sunset and never stopped till I hit the desert. It felt like home. I looked at all those fragile cactus, at those naked rocks sticking up like my own bones, and I said, "This is it. This is where I live."

Only I couldn't live in a fancy hotel or in one of the big cities. Professors like Robert travel a lot to conferences where they eat well, stroke and steal each other's inventions, and gossip, while their wives shop, take tours, and indulge in their own style of gossip. Sooner or later, I'd be found.

So I scouted around out in the bush and found what reminded me of a hobo camp in the Depression, except that there were women, too; nice women who smiled and offered me coffee cooked over a wood fire or a propane burner. They didn't ask me any questions, and I didn't question them, either. I went out, traded the Caddy to an Indian used car dealer for this pickup and little trailer that looks like a mushroom, and set up housekeeping. Me and the Hippie. I found him at the side of the road squatting in a pile of weeds, and I thought he was a Yorkshire terrier until he started to grow. He turned out mostly Irish wolfhound. A big difference, but he's good company and keeps strangers away.

What do I do with myself? I keep this journal. I hike. The Hippie and I have covered the washes, the valley, the sides of the mountains. I walk with a book of birds or flowers in my hand so I can learn the names of things. Once you learn what something is called, you've got power over it. The Indians believed that, and the slaves in the South. They all had secret names that nobody knew, and that meant there was still a part of themselves that belonged to them and was free. That's why nobody here has a last name, or if they do, it's a made-up name, not their real one. I wonder, if I'd had another name, would it have helped me? If I'd told Robert that my name was a secret, that I was someone other than Lily, and that he was neurotic, would it have helped? I already know the answer. He'd have said everything was my fault.

I go to bed when I'm tired, and wake up when I feel like it. I watch the sun rise through the *paloverde* branches, and there's something about the beginning of day that leaves me breathless. First the night lifts off, slowly, and the trees and mountains take on their daytime shapes. The sky in the East turns green, then red, catching fire, burning hotter and hotter—red, orange, yellow-white—and just

when you think you can't stand the beauty or the sus-
pense, the whole sky cracks like an egg and the sun is
born, spilling down the canyons in a river of light.

Nights are different. Mysterious. Cold. Enchanted. When
I can't sleep I watch how earth changes in moonlight. The
tree casts a thousand tiny shadows. There is an owl hoot-
ing, and coyotes chuckling in the wash. When he hears
them, the Hippie pricks his ears and howls like he wants to
join them, except he hasn't been invited, and he's very polite. I'd like to tell him, "Go on! Run! Kill a rabbit. Find a
nice lady coyote, all yellow-eyed and sassy, and prance and
grin and make funny puppies."

I don't say it, though. There are too many orphans in the
world as it is. I'm glad Robert and I were childless. We'd
have made a mess between us, and who needs more mixed-
up kids? We can't handle the ones we've got.

I think a lot, too. I guess that's obvious. All the facts of
life I took for granted have come under the microscope.
There are as many of them as there are rocks on the desert, and as many evils lurking underneath. I've had to think
each accepted rule through from beginning to end, learning what's true for myself.

Take Loper, for example. Unless I miss my guess, he's
an ex-con or a prison escapee living in a place that's part
dugout, part tent, part tin cans laid sideways and glued together, with the unopened ends facing out. They catch the
light and shine in your eyes, making Loper hard to see
when he's sitting under the mesquite tree skinning rabbits
or cleaning his .45. Nobody sneaks up on Loper. He was
raised on an Indian reservation in Montana, and he learned
all the tricks.

When I first came, he walked up the trail early one evening carrying an old iron pot. He was the ugliest man I'd
ever seen, the kind my mother told me to run from if I was
so unlucky as to meet him in a deserted alley.

Most of his front teeth were missing; easy to see because he carried his lips in a kind of snarl that was supposed to be a smile. I knew this because the Hippie does

the same thing every once in a while; in fact, at that moment, he was doing a fine imitation.

"Nice night," Loper said, stopping two feet away and planting his legs like logs in the sand.

"Yes," I said, fascinated by seeking so many tattoos at close range. They streamed down his arms all the way to his knuckles; mermaids, cobras, sharks, poisonous orchids, God knows what.

"I made too much stew. It won't keep." He held out the pot and I could smell the savory contents. "Since you just come, I thought I'd be neighborly."

He reminded me of a rattlesnake. Poke him and he'd coil. Otherwise, he was fine. "Thanks," I said, disregarding all my mother's edicts. "Want some coffee?"

"Naw. Too hot. I'd take a beer if you got one."

"Sorry," I said. "I'll stock up in town in a few days."

"Beer's the thing," he said. "Keeps down the dust." He turned and started down the trail, then stopped. "I'm just down here when you're done with the pot."

He looked like he felt foolish. Like he'd overstepped some invisible boundary. Surely a man like this one didn't worry about things like that?

"My name's Lily," I said.

His eyes brightened. "Loper," he said. "That's me." He rumpled the Hippie's fur. "Who's the mutt?"

"The Hippie. I found him in the weeds a couple months ago. Somebody must've dropped him."

He stared at me with those green glass eyes. "Lord," I thought. "He's a killer."

He said, "People suck."

"So what else is new?" I answered, and he laughed.

"Not too damn much," he said. "But it's nice, you keeping the dog." With that benediction, he bobbed his head and disappeared around the bend.

The stew was delicious. I wanted the recipe. The next morning I scrubbed the iron pot till the crust came off, called the Hippie, and went off down the path.

As I went I noticed bird tracks in the sand, quail, probably, and lots of coyote prints. I was studying the ground
when Loper materialized from behind a creosote bush and
stopped beside me.

"Lots of traffic last night," he said. "Lucky it wasn't the
Feds. How'd you like the stew?"

"Well enough to want the recipe."

He lifted his lip. "Well now," he said, "well now, I dunno.
You *sure* you liked it?"

"Sure I'm sure," I said, wondering what the catch was.
"What was in it? Rattlesnake?"

"Gophers," he said.

Fortunately I'd digested it all. I think I just turned white.

"I knew you'd puke if you knew what 'twas," he said.
"But you liked it, didn't you?"

I nodded, afraid to open my mouth.

"It's an Injun recipe. Had it since I was a kid. But it won't
do you no good 'less you can trap the gophers."

"Nevermind," I said. "Here's your pot. I cleaned it up."

He took it and looked at it like it was going to bite him.
"Damn," he said finally. "Took me years to get that flavor
on it."

"You mean that mess I scrubbed off?"

"Yeah, but don't worry. I got another."

"I'm sorry," I said. "I didn't mean to ruin it."

"Forget it. Your Ma raised you right."

I looked up into that fierce, ugly face. "Loper," I said,
"my Ma didn't raise me to know a single thing that counted."

"Hell, kid, she didn't know. She just thought she did like
everybody's Ma."

If that were true, then everybody had been or was in my
predicament; taking baby steps at age thirty-five, or maybe
never. If that were true, then we all raise ourselves, or
don't, and if we don't we find somebody who will. We
marry them and call them "husband" or "wife." The thought
was horrible. All evidence to the contrary, I'd married my
mother.

"I've got to go," I said. "Come by for a beer."

"I sure will." He tossed the pot in the brush and disappeared the way he'd come. It was uncanny how he was able to do that. I wanted to learn how, too. Maybe I'd need to disappear someday. I picked up the pot. It was a good one. Some things I learn fast.

I was sitting under the *paloverde* trying to convince myself that even though Robert had acted like a nagging mother it didn't mean I'd been guilty of incest, when a woman came up the trail, all arms, legs, and a braid of hair hanging over one shoulder.

"Howdy," she said, looking around and appraising my trailer.

I'd never said "howdy" to a living soul. I thought only movie cowboys talked like that. I repeated the greeting and hoped I didn't sound like a dude. I was after protective coloration.

"Loper said you moved in. I'm Meggie."

"Lily."

"Nice to·meet you." She stooped and let the Hippie smell her hand. "Loper said you were a real lady."

There was that word again. Even ex-cons seemed fond of it. "Is that good or bad, do you think?"

"Depends," she said. "You have a spare cigarette?"

I tossed her my pack. "Keep them if you're out."

She ran her fingers over the top of her head like she was plucking out her brains. "I'm trying to quit," she confessed. "I really am. But honest to God, it's hard. Maybe I shouldn't. What do you think?"

I'd been through that struggle. "Everybody's got to go some way. Dealer's choice."

"Now that's a fact. That's a real fact." She lit up, inhaled, exhaled, and watched the smoke rise through the tiny green twigs. Then she grinned. "You've convinced me, kid. I might die horny, but I'll be damned if I'll go wanting a smoke."

We sat awhile in silence, looking at the sky. Then she tucked the pack inside her T-shirt. "I'll pay you back on pay day," she said. "See you around. I'm just past Loper's if you need anything. Us women should stick together."

"Yeah," I answered, not wanting anything to do with women.

I was still stuck on the mother question. Maybe Robert had thought I was *his* mother, that old harridan who'd moved in on us and finally died in our third floor bedroom out of pure malice. It was hell getting her body down the narrow back stairs.

Did all this make me a creep? I wasn't sure. I'm still not sure. After all, morons can't know they're morons, so how can creeps tell?

Pondering all these matters got me through the summer and into the fall. Gradually I met the rest of the camp dwellers: Lorene and Carl who are married, dress alike in ragged roadrunner T-shirts and caps labeled "The Old Fart" and "The Old Fart's Wife"; the man we call "Father Frank," because he feeds the birds and they're always around him flashing their wings like biblical doves. Personally, I think he's a runaway priest, having seen him pacing back and forth like he's saying Angelus, and having noted in his dark eyes a reserve typical of all the priests I ever knew. As in, "Don't touch me. I'm holy." I always believed I could talk to God all by myself without using anyone else as a medium. I still believe it. Out here on the desert I talk to God every day. Like the Indians, I believe He's in the wind, the sky, the mountains. It makes it easy to pray.

This brings me to the medicine man, Jim Turtle, who walks around shirtless and who's usually out in a canyon meditating over a tin can filled with burning herbs or smoking on a pipe decorated with beads and eagle feathers. I stopped one day, mostly because I was tired of talking to myself and because he'd aroused my curiosity.

"Howdy," I said, congratulating myself. I sounded good. Like a native.

He turned and focused on me like I was five miles away. He said, "How."

Indians don't really say that, or if they do, they shouldn't. Coming from him, it sounded hokey. I sniffed the aroma of herbs and asked. "What're you smoking?"

"You want a drag, white woman?" he answered.

I could hear my mother's voice loud and clear. For once, she was right. "I've got to go," I said. "No thanks."

"You look like you got problems. You want to go in the sweat lodge, you come tell me. Jim Turtle." He smiled, looking purely evil.

"You watch out for him," Loper said when I repeated the conversation. "He's bad medicine. Attracts women like a pile of manure brings flies."

"That doesn't sound nice," I said, picturing the event and recalling how, in childhood, no one ever talked about manure.

"It ain't supposed to. I grew up with Injuns, and he's a bad one if he even is an Injun. I bet he's from Brooklyn."

"Now how would you know that?" I asked.

"I was in the Navy."

"What's that got to do with it?"

"Stationed in Brooklyn," he said.

Out of some deep-rooted desire for mischief, I said, "He asked me to go in his sweat lodge."

Loper's eyes went that hard, killer green. "I'll sweat lodge him. Don't you go."

"I never intended to. I just thought it was funny."

"Ha," he said without humor. "If he bothers you again, you tell me."

"He didn't bother me. I just asked what was he smoking."

Loper threw up his hands. "Don't you know better than to go around asking guys that? You're a damn fool, and that's the truth."

Actually, I didn't know better. When it comes to people like these, I'm as green as the trunk of the *paloverde*. "Common," my mother would have called them, dismissing in two syllables the possibility that they bore any resemblance to her own person or to mine.

I'm beginning to pity her. She missed out on the fun.

These people are fun. Alive. Vital. Interesting, even though they stick to the brush like quail. Better that than inside a twelve-room house decorated by some fag according to his taste and not mine. Better out here than almost anything I can think of.

What makes a home? It isn't necessarily four walls and a roof. Jim Turtle sleeps in a wickiup; the priest in a blue canvas tent. And I read recently about a bag lady who refused to leave her beat and go into a shelter. She said she liked her life the way it was.

As for me, I've put down roots like a desert plant; down through layers of sand and rock to where the water runs cold and clear, only the roots exist in my mind, not in the place. I could live anywhere, and I guess I'll have to.

Right after Thanksgiving, which came and went without anybody noticing because people on food stamps aren't much into holidays, Jim Turtle began digging into the crumbling banks of the wash just like his namesake. He made a kind of dugout that he roofed over and fronted with yucca stalks and weeds, and then he carried rocks inside—big ones, big enough to rupture most men. He didn't seem to notice their size, just flexed his muscles and kept humming to himself.

I found him sitting beside his little room one day when I was coming back from a walk. I wouldn't have seen him except that the Hippie's hackles went up and he started to growl. That dog hated Jim, for what reason I didn't know, except that Loper said dogs have an instinct about people, and the Hippie knew Jim was no good.

"What's that you built?" I asked out of simple politeness. My upbringing again. Always be nice to people.

He tipped his head back to see me better as I stood above him. "Sweat lodge," he said. "Some folks in town want to try it. You can try, too. Just come on down. Leave the mutt at home." He started to get up. The Hippie growled harder.

"That dog's nuts. You know that?"

"He's okay."

"Woman like you needs a real dog."

That put my back up. What did he know about dogs or about women like me? I smiled my most condescending smile learned at my mother's knee.

"Smart ass," he said and sat down with his back to me.

"Dumb son of a bitch," I yelled at his head.

Loper materialized out of a cactus a few yards further on. "Now that's real nice. You sound like you grew up in a pool hall."

It was happening again—the remaking of Lily. I freaked out. "Who're you? My mother?"

"Somebody's got to keep you out of trouble."

"I can take care of myself."

"Yeah," he said. "What'll you do when you wake up some night and find him in your bunk?"

"He wouldn't dare."

Loper raised his lip. "Don't count on it, sweetheart," he said.

I went fuming to Meggie's. "I thought people out here minded their own business. It seems like everybody's minding mine."

She drew a bead on me with her blue eyes. "Hell, kid," she said. "They've never seen anybody like you before."

Didn't I fit anywhere? Was I always going to be out of place? "What's so different about me?" I cried. "I'm just me."

"Like Loper said, you're a lady." She lit a cigarette and waved it at me, cutting off my protest. "Calm down and listen. You come in here and expected to have it all your own way, but nobody has it like that, not even here. You're young, you've got money or seem to, and you're pretty. What'd you expect with a bunch of horny guys, a serenade? They're snuffing your tracks like a bunch of hounds, Loper included, and they can't help it. The trouble with men is women. And vice versa."

I grasped at the one word that made sense. "I'm not pretty," I said. I believed that to be true. No one had ever commented one way or the other on my looks, probably guarding me from conceit. Even Robert in the sentimental days before our marriage had remained silent on the subject. His one flattering remark, if such it was, was that I had nice arms.

Meggie snorted. "Oh, Lord, look in the mirror!" She had a small glass tacked on the wall, and she pushed me at it.

I looked and saw my face. Eyes, nose, mouth, all in a line like everybody else's. I shrugged. "Nobody's making sense around here. Not even you."

She backed off, belligerent as a cat. "You don't think?"

"No. All I see is everybody with a finger in my pie, and I've had that up to here."

"Well now," she said, drawing herself up, "well now, you go ahead and do it on your own then, you know so much. Only don't come running to me every time you want answers."

So I went home, and a week passed without my seeing a soul. I caught glimpses of the others, but they were shy as rabbits and kept to themselves. By the end of the second week, I was lonesome. I hadn't talked to anybody but the Hippie, and he never answered. So I was almost glad to see Jim Turtle coming through the mesquite toward me. The sunlight gleamed on that chest of his like he'd painted himself with bronze oil. He probably had. Close up he looked like a collage with parts added here and there. Even his braid seemed like an afterthought.

He showed his white teeth. "How," he said.

The Hippie rumbled in his throat, and his eyes, focused on Jim's belly button, looked like an alligator's.

Hoping to keep him at a distance, I said, "Yes?"

He steam rolled right over my fragile barrier. Ladylike behavior had no effect on him. "How'd you like your picture in the paper?"

All I could think of was Robert's reaction if he should see me, Lily, on the front page surrounded by half-naked oddballs. "No thanks," I said. "I take terrible pictures."

He snickered and squatted down and drew lines in the sand with his finger. "They want to write about my sweat lodge in the paper. I thought it'd look good, you standing out front."

"There must be a lot of women you could ask," I said. "You don't need me."

He stopped drawing and looked right at me. "But you got yellow hair." He sounded wistful, like a kid full of dreams.

I thought fast. He probably pulled that sad act on all the girls. I looked back into those bottomless dark eyes. "Why don't you put an ad in the paper?"

He was on his feet in one fluid motion. "You think you're so cool," he snarled, "coming in here like Mrs. Socialite slumming." Then he reached out and grabbed a handful of my hair right below my ear.

The Hippie went for his arm. I opened my mouth and yelled like a Comanche, and when he loosened his hold I grabbed Loper's old pot and clobbered him. I missed knocking him out—he was quick—but I connected with his ribs until the pot rang like a church bell.

He was backing down the trail as fast as he could with the Hippie hanging onto his leg and me swinging away when Loper charged up and wrapped a tattooed arm around his neck. He dragged him around the bend with the dog still clinging. It was hard to tell who was growling loudest.

I was ready to follow and finish what I'd started when the shock hit me. Not the kind of shock you'd expect, either. I wanted to kick him, gouge out his eyes, yell over the body. I could feel the blood in my veins, the heat of the red earth in the soles of my feet. Strength boiled up inside like a lava flow, and suddenly and completely I understood why men love war and struggle to climb mountains. At the same point I wondered what was wrong with me and all the women I'd known who trembled at harsh words and hid under the bed at the smallest sign of violence. Where had all the Amazons gone?

I threw back my head and laughed. I was alive. Life was precious. So was I. I was still laughing when Loper came back blowing on his knuckles.

"You did good, kid," he said. Then he squinted at me. "You hysterical or something?"

"Nope," I answered.

The Hippie ran past us with what looked like a black-snake trailing from his jaws. Loper gestured with his thumb. "He got the scalp. Didn't I tell you he was a fake? His hair's red as Bridie Murphy's."

"Let's have a beer," I said, wanting to celebrate my new-found strength.

We sat awhile in silence, drinking and absorbing the sun like a couple of lizards. Then he said, "I reckon you found out some things today your Ma never told you."

"I guess I've been hiding out most of my life."

He drained his beer and opened a second. "Better late than never as they say."

Around us the desert shimmered with light and the sway-ing of branches. From one of them a thrasher whistled, "Phew!" like a come-on, and in the distance another an-swered. Like the pied piper, they seemed to be calling me.

I said, "I wish I could stay."

"Hell, kid. You got things to do with your life. The rest of us have kinda run out of gas."

I stared at the mountains that ringed the horizon. Beyond them was more desert; other mountains lifted their shoul-ders in the distance, and beyond them was California with its movie stars and earthquakes, and hippies who read poetry in coffee houses, smoked dope, slept around. I had never slept around. I didn't know how to begin. It seemed I knew less now than I had when I started.

The little encampment had become home even if its people were has-beens. All I could say for myself was that I had never been at all. "Loper," I said, "it's big out there."

His eyes went hard, then soft again. "I'm bettin' on you," was all he said.

"I'll miss you." That was the truth. Leaving Loper was harder than leaving Robert had been.

Sentiment didn't sit easy on Loper. He looked like he wanted to be someplace else. He grunted.

"I'll tell you what," I said, grasping at straws, hating to cut my traces. "Live in my trailer. That way I'll know there's a place to come home to."

He grunted again and emptied the bottle. "Sure kid, if that's what you want. But you won't be back. Just go on and keep your nose clean." He got up, ruffled my hair the same way he ruffled the Hippie's, and went off down the trail.

Now I'm loaded up and ready to go. The Hippie's riding shotgun. I'm touching the *paloverde* tree like I can take it with me—green, thorny, tough. I'm looking at the blue cloud shadows, the heat waves dancing in the air, the red earth, and I'm feeling the way the pioneers must have felt heading West. The women, too. They didn't get here by pulling fainting spells, putting on airs, worrying about the neighbors. They had more important things to think about. Like living. They did what they had to do, and if they shed tears over being uprooted and leaving loved ones, they did it in silence, inside where no one could see. In their pockets they carried seeds to plant to remind them of home.

I pick a pod from the tree. It is boat-shaped like a dry pea, and inside it the seeds shiver when shaken. I put it in my shirt pocket, get in the truck, and slam the door.

Call me Lily Appleseed, off to make a little history of my own.

A Note about the Author

Jane Candia Coleman was the co-founder and Director of the Womens' Creative Writing Center at Carlow College in Pittsburgh, Pennsylvania. She now lives on a ranch near Rodeo, New Mexico with four horses, eight dogs, and too many cats to count. She is the author of "No Roof But Sky," a collection of poetry awarded the National Cowboy Hall of Fame's Western Heritage Award for 1990, "The Voices of Doves," a fiction chapbook, and "Shadows in My Hands," personal essays about the Southwest.